WHITEHORSE

JIM FRISHKEY

ISBN: 9781540849274

Cover design by Susan Asbill
Axeman Press

WHITEHORSE

JIM FRISHKEY

To the brave members of the Mashantuket Pequots, a small tribe in Connecticut, who stood strong against Donald J. Trump's harassment and law suits. Today their Foxwoods Casino continues to generate significant income and is a resounding success. Mr. Trump's casinos failed and went bankrupt.

CHAPTER 1

November, 1968:

Somewhere outside of Hue, South Vietnam

As the extraction helicopter descended, Spec Four Billy Whitehorse watched as the lead man was cut down just as he reached the pick-up zone. Looking back, he could not be certain if his Ranger training took over or a simple surge of pure adrenalin kicked in as he quickly rose and delivered a steady stream of suppressing fire on the attackers while other team members pulled the wounded man back to safety.

After administering what first aid he could to the soldier, he had the team load their comrade on to the helicopter. Simultaneously, a mortar round ripped into the group, instantly killing three men and wounding all the others. Despite the wounds he sustained from the blast, Whitehorse rushed from man to man, giving what aid he could, including heart massage. He then called in tactical air strikes on the enemy's positions, allowing additional rescue choppers to land and remove the remaining wounded. Whitehorse remained on the ground until friendly reinforcements arrived.

For his actions that day, Billy Whitehorse became one of the most decorated American soldiers of the Vietnam War. He was awarded the Distinguished Service Cross; three Silver Stars; six Bronze Stars and five Purple Hearts. By any reasonable person's measure…he was an American Hero. To most, he was just an Indian.

Billy was eventually discharged as a First Lieutenant…58th Infantry; 101st Airborne; Army Rangers. Like many others who returned from that war, Billy had no idea what the effects of Agent Orange might have on his life.

* * *

April, 1988: Las Vegas, Nevada

Wilfred Drummond loved to build things, a passion now shared by his oldest son Damon. Drummond Construction's many projects were towering symbols of luxury in many of the largest cities across the country. Nothing came easy to Wilfred as he amassed his fortune but, like many parents from the greatest generation, he failed to pass the virtue of earned wealth to his pampered son. Instead, he used his money and influence to provide Damon with a security blanket…a level of privilege not available to the little people. And Damon smothered himself in the gifts his father provided.

No one liked Damon, but his wealth attracted the ambulance chasers who lined up to get a small piece of the action. He bounced from one private school to another, trying the patience of the system until he got tossed out on his ear. With the Vietnam War heating up, Wilfred knew his son could never survive getting drafted and going off to battle. A friendly doctor and greedy member of the draft board got Daman a physical deferment and the spoiled playboy watched the war from his television.

Later when Damon expressed a serious interest in joining his father's company, Wilfred insisted that his son prove himself and enrolled him into the UNLV Lee Business School MBA Program. How he got him accepted is subject to speculation but the University was always grateful for major endowment contributions by prominent members of the community.

Damon chose to focus his studies on New Venture Management which added courses in "Venture Feasibility and Creation" and "Negotiation" to the standard MBA course load. He was a natural. He sailed through the course work and excelled in leading the seminars on Negotiations. He learned that making a deal could be an art form and that the only bad deal was the one you didn't make. In spite of his latent success in academia, he could not shake his reputation as an arrogant asshole…one that would stick with him his entire life.

Although Drummond Construction Group was headquartered in Dallas, Damon always felt too cosmopolitan for life in the wild west and, after graduating from UNLV, he took a strong interest in the Vegas glitz and glamor and began to seek out projects that would allow him to remain there. First on his list was roping in some hot showgirls. He was on his way.

The Drummond office in Las Vegas was relatively small, located in a one story building on North Rancho Drive. All of their projects thus far were of medium size, specializing in structural steel and metal buildings. The permanent staff was lean in size which helped make this division one of the most profitable in the entire Drummond Group. Mark Beauville was the manager and his sister Jill ran the office.

Mark was around Damon's age and had worked for the company seven years…all in Las Vegas. When he got word that the owner's son, whom many described as a whiny little bitch, would be officing with him he was ready to quit the company. "Don't do anything stupid," his sister told him when she heard the news. “Form your own opinion then do what you think is best and if you leave…I’ll be right behind you.”

Despite his massive ego, Damon spent the first few weeks observing and travelling the city talking to members of the Chamber of Commerce and Gaming Commission. When he called his father to request a meeting in Dallas, he had a game plan and wanted permission to move forward.

Wilfred was impressed with the newly discovered sense of responsibility that his son was displaying. When Damon asked for a sit-down Wilfred had an idea what the boy had in mind and was eager to hear what he had to say. He sent the company plane to McCarran immediately.

* * *

The flight to Dallas Love Field was short and the company limo was waiting on the tarmac when the corporate jet rolled to a stop. “Welcome back, Sir,” the driver greeted him as he climbed in. “You picked a lovely day for your visit.” Damon smiled politely but said nothing on the drive to the lavish corporate center on McKinney Avenue.

The lobby receptionist announced Damon’s arrival and he was instructed to take the elevator to the 30th floor where the executive suites were located. “Good afternoon

Mister Drummond. Your father is waiting for you in the conference room." His greeter was one of a dozen young and beautiful staffers that worked their way through the Drummond system…none staying very long but all achieving the highest level of tolerance for office-place harassment.

As Damon entered the mahogany paneled room, he realized for the first time that his father was aging. Wilfred looked small and frail sitting at the long conference table…empty except for the lone man who stood to greet his son. "Hello father. Thanks for seeing me on such short notice." He walked around the table and gave his father a hug that was lacking any warmth. Just a traditional and expected greeting for the man who covered the bills.

Wilfred had a leather portfolio laying on the table in front of him. "Have a seat son. Before we get to your agenda I wanted to go over a few things with you…specifically your activities in Las Vegas since you joined the company."

"Oh fuck!" Damon thought as he took his seat and poured a glass of ice water. "Please spare me another bitch session. I have important things to discuss with you."

"On the contrary, son. I am very pleased with your efforts since getting your MBA. Your co-workers have had nothing but good things to say about you. No police files have come to my attention and, I trust, there are no show girls running around carrying your baby." His father smiled…a rare display of emotion and Damon relaxed.

"I've turned a corner father," Damon began. "I want to take the company to another level. Instead of just building projects for others, I want to develop and market future projects under our own brand…the Drummond brand."

Wilfred knew what was coming. Mark Beauville had called him when Damon left for the airport. "Mr. Drummond. I apologize for contacting you direct but I thought you needed to know why Damon is flying in." He went on to explain the meetings Damon was having with the locally owned casinos…picking their brains but vowing never to become a competitor. "I'm pretty sure he wants to build his own casino. Might not be a bad idea as long as we can hold on to our existing customers."

Wilfred listened carefully but did not comment. "Thank you for the call Mark, and say hello to your lovely sister." End of conversation.

CHAPTER 3

Damon finished his presentation and waited for his father's comments. "Well, what do you think?"

"That is a very ambitious undertaking you are proposing," his father began. "And very expensive, it appears. Our company has never sought to develop a brand for good reason. It requires a massive investment and usually doesn't make money. Our reputation is based upon providing cost effective, quality structures for blue chip customers, and it has served us very well thus far."

Damon was not having it. "And that is exactly why we need to look at the future and take bold steps like what I am proposing. Let's eliminate the middle men and go directly to the consumer where the big money is. Let's take advantage of the strong reputation we have created. The Drummond name will be on a level with the finest brands in the world, and it will start with the Drummond Hotel and Casino."

Wilfred had prepared for this moment after his conversation with Mark. He reached into his desk drawer and pulled out an envelope which he slid across the table to his son. Damon took the envelope and opened it, inspecting the check it contained…$1 million dollars payable to Damon Drummond.

"What is this?" he asked.

Winfred sat back and smiled. "It is your seed money for this fantasy you want to pursue. That is the company's total and only investment we will make. You are on your own. You can use our offices as a headquarters and I will instruct our team to support you with advice if you want it. The only condition is that you do nothing to damage our name…nothing. Understood?"

Damon didn't know what to say. This was clearly not what he wanted nor expected. He knew for sure that this would not be enough to fund a casino construction, let alone pay for the land to build it on. "That's very generous father but I need a hell of a lot more than that to create what I described to you. I'm guessing around $60 million."

"Please understand son, I think your idea is a loser but I gave you something you can build upon if you really believe in this thing. My offer is final and remember, if I discover you pissed this money away on anything else, your career will be over. Have a safe flight back to Vegas." Winfred pressed a button and his secretary entered his office. "Sally please show my son to the private elevator."

Damon followed the secretary to the lobby and he rode the private elevator to the first floor where a limo had been summoned and was waiting. "Take me to the Anatole. The plane can wait."

Over the years Damon had found the courtyard bar at the Anatole Hotel a great place to find women…and one in particular was a cocktail waitress named Elena. She had entered the country from the Czech Republic as a young girl and her beauty helped launch a struggling modeling career. Dallas was growing as a fashion hub but still a long way from the runways of New York and Europe. Waiting for the next shoot required a job and she settled in nicely at the Anatole.

When Damon was in town, he always tried to find his way to her and a relationship began to grow…mostly sexual although he kept coming back, many times just for conversations over drinks. Today would be one of those visits as he had to get back to Vegas to plan his next move.

As always, Elena was busy moving from one table to another with trays of drinks and nuts to keep the patrons dry and thirsty. She didn't notice Damon as he walked across the atrium lobby and took a seat at the bar. "Hey, can a guy get a drink around here?" he called out as she walked by. "Another obnoxious Texan" she thought until she looked up and saw Damon smiling that stupid grin she came to like.

"Well hello stranger. What brings you to town? It certainly isn't to see little old me." She placed a napkin in front of him and fetched his favorite tequila shot. He motioned for her to take the stool next to him which she did as the bar was virtually empty at mid-day.

"I missed you Elena. It gets lonely in Vegas despite the hectic atmosphere." She was seeing a rare moment of sincerity. Without thinking he continued. "How would you like to spend a long weekend with me. The plane is waiting for us right now."

"You are crazy!" she replied. "I have a job. I can't just walk out like that."

Damon was now locked in on this impromptu idea. "Sure you can. And we can get you some clothes when we arrive. You never know. Lots of agents and producers are running around that town and one may take an interest in you. In fact, there is probably a good chance you won't want to go back to Dallas."

Elena was trying to read between the lines. She came to this country as the daughter of a peasant family with little formal education. Still, she was a good judge of people and her heart was telling her to take a gamble on this guy. He was rich, good looking and treated her with respect. Really, she had nothing to lose.

"You are a nut but I need some adventure in my life. OK, let's do this." She looked around the bar area for the manager but he was not around. She grabbed a cocktail napkin and hastily scribbled her resignation and left it on the bar. Damon grabbed her hand and they headed to the waiting limo.

* * *

Since Damon returned from Dallas with Elena, he decided to move to a penthouse in the Las Vegas Hilton. The rent was outrageous but Elena was blown away, the real reason he went overboard. He didn't tell his father but knew it would only be a matter of time until word got to him...probably from Mark Beauville.

True to his word, Damon did his best to land a modeling job for Elena but simply didn't have the contacts to pull it off. The best he could do was get her an audition for the chorus line at the Riviera. She rejected the idea at first but considered the life she had left as a bar maid and decided to give it a shot. She had everything they were looking for...she was tall, thin and moved like a swan. Her starting salary was $750 per week and could go up if the number of shows she appeared in increased.

In reality, Elena didn't need to work. Damon was paying for everything and she could spend her days at the slots and the pool if she chose. Her peasant roots prevented her from going soft so she threw herself into her work, practicing the routines until she could perform them in her sleep. Her work ethic did not go unnoticed and in a few weeks, she was elevated to one of the lead dancers which also got her a raise in salary, but less time to be with Damon.

* * *

If any one person could be called the King of Las Vegas it would be Aubrey Bennison. The billionaire owned three of the newest and most luxurious hotels on the strip and his money funded many a conservative political campaign. His wallet was open to the right cause or person but not without significant costs to those who kissed his ring. Rumors persisted that he had several high-ranking senators, governors and members of congress deep into his pocket and the current Republican President had a huge IOU that could be called in at any time for favors or more.

Although he was headquartered in Las Vegas, Bennison's vast holdings propelled him across the globe. When Damon decided to reach out to him he was in flight to Singapore to close a deal on building a new casino resort in Marina Cove. He took Damon's call because he recognized and respected his father and what he built from nothing…like Aubrey did himself.

"How can I help you?" Bennison answered. The private jet was as quiet as a church and the caller would have never known he was talking to someone at 30,000 feet.

"Mister Bennison, this is Damon Drummond. May I call you Aubrey?"

"No you may not," came the terse reply. "I'm a busy man, sonny. What do you want?"

Damon was not used to being treated like this but he wanted something that this man had lots of…money. "I'm sorry, sir. I don't want to waste your time so I'll get to the point.".

"Please do," Aubrey replied.

"I have recently met with my father and we are beginning to line up investors for a new and exciting project for the Drummond Group…a spectacular new Nevada resort and casino."

"Are you a fucking idiot?" Bennison answered in disbelief. "You are calling to tell me you are becoming a direct competitor in my own backyard? Go back and tell your father I will crush you small-time bottom dwellers and make the Drummond name a joke."

"Please, Mr. Bennison, let me finish before you draw the wrong conclusion. This new project will not be in Las Vegas nor anywhere remotely close to any of your locations. This is an iron clad promise we will back up in writing if you like."

Bennison was getting even more annoyed. "Listen sonny. I really don't give a shit what you do or where you do it. You want to take me on in Vegas?...have at it. Now go away."

"Will you at least let me lay out our plan in person? You like making money…this will be a cash cow for you, believe me. It will be huge." Damon was begging and didn't like it one bit.

Bennison liked the kid's balls and decided it wouldn't cost him anything to give him a meeting. "OK, you wore me out. I'll be back in Vegas in a few days. Call me then and we'll arrange a time to meet."

It took Damon six calls before he got through to Bennison's secretary. As was customary, she said her boss was in a meeting and unavailable. "Bullshit!" Damon answered. "I'm calling him for a meeting just as he asked me to do. And I want that meeting now."

She put him on hold and almost ten minutes later he heard the big man's voice. "You're a rude little prick aren't you. If you ever talk to one of my people like that again you will be cleaning out the toilets in one of my casinos."

"I'm sorry but patience is not one of my virtues," Damon replied. "I'm just following up for a meeting like you told me to do. It's been almost three weeks."

"Get your ass over here in thirty minutes," Aubrey answered. "I'll give you one hour. Don't waste it."

It was a short drive down the Strip but Damon chose to flag a cab and save time. Bennison's private office was in the basement of the Convention Center. The security was like a maximum-security prison with check points manned by heavily armed guards. After identifying himself numerous times with various forms of identification, Damon entered the reception area. The opulence was overwhelming. Gold, marble, imported tapestries and precious artifacts from ancient civilizations adorned the décor. Damon knew he was seeing the top of the food chain for luxury and personal wealth.

"You may go right in Mister Drummond," the matronly secretary instructed and Damon opened the expansive double doors into the private sanctuary of one of the wealthiest men on the planet.

"Sit down kid. Let's get right to business. I'll have one of the girls give you the grand tour on your way out." Bennison was not a big man and sitting behind the massive desk made him look even smaller.

"Mister Bennison, I need $60 million. The Drummond Group believes there is a great opportunity to build a casino resort in Laughlin, right on the river. It will draw from three adjacent states without impacting the overall business in Vegas. It will attract locals from Phoenix with RV's who don't want to fight the congestion on the Strip and we will provide a large area just for motor homes with power and water hookups."

"Your old man has plenty of money, why do you need my help?" Bennison was curious and maybe even a little interested.

"Two reasons," Damon answered. "First, we know nothing about the gaming industry and you know everything. Having access to your knowledge and connections would be invaluable. Second, I want to do this on my own. My father has provided me with some seed money but is drawing the line there. He is not totally comfortable yet with the idea but he will jump on board once I prove I can get it off the ground."

Bennison started to laugh, infuriating Damon who's face started to turn red. "Kid, you must have missed some classes in grad school. We've looked at Laughlin and the best site that could accommodate a sizeable resort is owned by the Indians…and they ain't selling. You're wasting my time. I'm an idiot for taking you seriously. Have a nice day." He buzzed for his secretary. "Show Mister Drummond out please…and skip the tour."

Damon was speechless as he followed the secretary to the elevator up to the main floor. Bennison was right. The tribal land was the best location but not the only one. There were several acres adjacent to the reservation property that was available and Damon could use the money from his father to lock it down. Once he had the land in his pocket Bennison would come to the table.

CHAPTER 4

Two years later

The SEMA Show brought neither the largest nor the most generous group of conventioneers to the city, but they were eager to consume cheap booze in the many lounges spread up and down the Strip. Willy Deville's band finished their final set with a generous gathering of these party goers still on hand at last call. Billy Whitehorse was the lead guitarist and left it all out on the stage that night. It was his fortieth birthday and, like every other day, he would be alone, miles away from his family in Oklahoma.

The band was facing an open week without any bookings and Billy was looking forward to just kicking back and laying by the pool. He loaded his gear into his trusty 1982 Trans Am and made the short drive to his one-bedroom apartment. After unloading his Marshall and Les Paul, he opened a beer and crashed on the couch where he would wake up the following afternoon.

Despite his lofty status as a war hero, Billy returned from Nam as just another out of work Indian destined for the reservation where his family had status as tribal leaders of the Cherokees of the Red Bison Clan. His father had attended Oklahoma State and received an MBA. His education was put to good use in managing the finances of the Tribe and his personal wealth was equal to any white business man of the area.

Billy had many opportunities to work for the tribe but had few friends. His war record carried little weight within the reservation, but found no one who he could share his feelings with…no one who had similar experiences with the horrors of combat. Regular sessions with the VA shrinks had no impact. Instead, he filled his hours practicing on the guitar, a skill he found came naturally and provided the perfect escape.

After many months, he finally thought he would showcase his talent to a real crowd and drove to Tulsa. After visiting several bars with live music, the Willy Deville Show Band let him sit in after closing one night. He loved their song list, sprinkled with Blues, Funk and Rock, and he made Deville sit up and take notice. An offer to join the band on the road was accepted and he soon left the reservation and nightmares of war in his rear-view mirror.

Sitting in his apartment 10 years later, Billy was still alone. Even with a growing stable of show girls and casino waitresses, he had never found anyone close to what he envisioned a life partner would be. He needed to quit thinking.

The Vista Del Valle Apartments was a short walk from Billy's favorite coffee shop in the Gold Coast Casino and he found walking in the crisp night air cleared his brain. He grabbed the early edition of the Las Vegas Review-Journal and took his usual seat in a booth as far from the casino floor as possible. He was still hungry from the late-night gig and ordered his favorite chicken-fried steak and eggs which he consumed almost without taking a breath.

After a refill of his coffee, Billy lit his first Marlboro of the day and opened the paper. He had nothing but time and settled in to reading each section of the paper. Nothing particularly stimulating in the Sports section but an article from the national section made him sit up and take notice. Congress had just passed into law the Indian Gaming Regulatory Act which allowed that any form of gambling allowed by the states must be permitted on a reservation. He knew his father had spent considerable time and tribal money lobbying in Washington for this law's passage. For many years, they had quietly set aside the land and resources needed to build a casino. That time had finally arrived.

"Hey Pop. Just read about the passage of the Gaming law. Congratulations!" Billy hadn't talked to his family for several months but knew how important this was and wanted to weigh in with his support.

Wilson Whitehorse was a proud chief…a warrior in the heritage of Chief John Ross who opposed the treaty which led to the "Trail of Tears" in 1838 when 4,000 Cherokee died of hunger, exposure and disease. His education and status did not cloud the memories of his heritage and he never trusted the white man…even with a signed document.

Wilson was proud of his son's military service but never spoke of it. Service to the white man was not an achievement admired by those who suffered the most at their hands. He often thought how great it would be to have his son standing proudly by his side when he traveled to Washington. Sadly, that was not to be.

"Thank you Billy. It was a long and expensive fight. You are well I assume? Oh yes, happy birthday. Forty is a milestone for our people."

Billy thought his father sounded very tired. "Yeah, I'm doing OK," Billy answered. "I've got a week off. Thought I might come see you and Mom." This was not planned but just seemed like the right thing to do now that he had his father on the phone.

"Suit yourself. I have meetings scheduled all week with architects and the state gaming commission. You are welcome to sit in if you like." In his own way, Wilson was happy his son was coming to visit.

Billy was not looking forward to the sixteen-hour drive to Tulsa. He loved his car but it was a bar-hopper, not suited to cross-country commutes. After checking schedules and prices he decided to fly to Tulsa…a 2 ½ hour flight with no stops. Once he landed he would either call the reservation for a ride or rent a car.

Billy caught some much-needed sleep during the flight and arrived in Tulsa where the heat was almost as stifling as Vegas. He grabbed his carry-on and sought out the rental car counters, deciding it best to have some independence if his visit went south. He could always drive to a motel if necessary.

It was a short drive to the home of his father and he could sense the change as he crossed into reservation land. Maybe it was the ghosts of his ancestors watching as he travelled the dusty tundra that was his tribe's final stop in a long and bloody trail of tears.

Since he left to pursue his music, the tribal landscape had improved dramatically. Gone were the broken pickups that littered the streets and homesteads. New businesses had popped up including a new Starbucks…one of the first to be built in the state. The tribal council headquarters was newly constructed and adjacent to the police station and fire house. That was where his father had his office and where Billy would find him this day.

Billy parked his rental car in front of the gift shop, who's windows were filled with the usual tourist souvenirs of blankets and turquoise jewelry. From behind the counter, a clerk noticed the man crossing the street to the Council Headquarters and her jaw dropped in disbelief. "Jesus, is that Billy Whitehorse?" she mumbled to herself.

Eva hadn't seen or heard from Billy since he left for greener pastures. Seeing him now rekindled old feelings that she had tried to suppress. As hard as she tried, she could not heal the scars Billy had sustained in Vietnam…the psychological ones that woke him up dripping in sweat most nights. She was his girl, but he needed more than she could provide…and it broke her heart.

She watched as he entered the building where his father worked and contemplated if she should reach out to him while he was in town. "He left me," she decided. If he wanted to see her he would find her.

Billy was greeted by a young receptionist who smiled politely. "How can I help you?" she asked. She was probably just out of high school but showed a refreshing abundance of confidence in her work environment.

"I'm here to see Wilson Whitehorse. I'm his son Billy. He's expecting me." The girl walked down a hall and minutes later returned with his father in tow. They embraced and then the father stepped back to take in the full picture of his offspring.

"You look very fit Billy. Still have the long hair I see but at least it's in a ponytail. Come let's go to my office." Billy followed his father who closed the door once Billy had taken a seat.

Billy was surprised that his father had adorned the walls with pictures of his son and clippings of his military honors from the local newspapers. Sitting in full view on the old man's desk were Billy's medals which he had eagerly given to his father once he returned home. He didn't need any reminders of the war. His head was filled with them.

"Your mother has planned a little impromptu birthday party for you while you are here. She has also cleaned your old room. Obviously you will be staying with us." This was an order not a request and Billy would have preferred keeping a safe distance from his family but he knew it would break his mother's heart if he didn't stay at the house.

"Of course. Sounds good to me," he answered. "So tell me about this project you have planned. A casino owned by the tribe. Who would have believed this could ever be a reality?"

Wilson retrieved some blue prints from behind his desk and laid them out on the nearby conference table. "Here are the plans, Billy. Take a look. The tentative name is "The Anisahoni Resort and Casino" …named after our Cherokee clan."

Billy rolled out the first of the large prints and studied the layouts with great interest. "Pretty darn big casino floor…even by Vegas standards. I see a separate room for poker and baccarat. Do you really think the tribe will get into baccarat?"

Wilson laughed. "If the patrons were only Indians I would agree with you but did you notice the location where we are building?" Billy read the site address out loud…" Nevada? Seriously?"

"Yes you are correct. As you know, the real money in gaming is in Las Vegas and the surrounding area. Oklahoma can draw from the Dallas area but local money is not consistent nor as great as the real tourist gamblers. That is why we are partnering with the Fort Mohave Tribe in Laughlin, to build our casino on the shores of the Colorado River. We will be nestled on the Nevada, Arizona and Colorado border. With everything we are planning, it will be a gamers paradise."

Billy continued inspecting the blue prints. He was particularly impressed with the Sports Book, live Bingo, Keno and more. "Very impressive. I see plans for a Private Beach and boat launch. And you came up with enough cash to get this thing built?"

"Yes...combining the resources of our two tribes will get us off and running. The rest of the money will come from private investors which we are now lining up. In fact, I have a meeting with them tomorrow. You are welcome to attend if you like."

The one thing Billy had become an expert observer of is Vegas gaming. Perhaps he could provide some firsthand knowledge at the meeting. "Sure, I'd like that."

"Great," Wilson said and stood to end the meeting. "I'll see you tonight. Don't forget about the party…and act surprised."

Billy walked back to his car, not noticing the eyes of his first love watching intently. She was invited to the party and hoped that Billy would accept her presence in the spirit of an old friend wishing him a happy birthday.

* * *

Billy was overwhelmed with the great smells of the food he grew up on. His cousins and aunts had prepared kanuchi, green chili slew, grape dumplings and creamed dandelion leaves. The family atmosphere was in full bloom…enjoying stories of Billy's youth and his sports accomplishments before he enlisted to go to war. No mention was made of what he had left behind until Eva arrived with homemade blueberry Wojabi, a perfect substitute for the white man's birthday cake.

"Hello Billy. Welcome home…and happy birthday." She looked as good as the day he jumped on the bus for basic training and when she hugged him, every moment they had shared came streaming back into his mind.

"Eva!" he offered sheepishly. "You haven't aged a bit and thank you for joining us." His disjointed comments revealed how much he had missed her but he would never say it out loud. She made the rounds, hugging his mother and father and the other relatives around the dinner table.

"Ready for desert?" she asked as she placed a large slab of fried bread in front of each person, then covered it with the lusciously sweet Wojabi. As they broke into "Happy Birthday", Billy had a sense that his life was about to take a hard turn away from his comfort zone.

After the celebration subsided, Billy went to the front porch and lit a Marlboro, amazed at the clarity of the night sky away from the big city lights. Alone, he was soon joined by Eva who had wrapped a shawl around her shoulders to combat the chill of the night air.

"I saw you this morning when you first arrived in town. I run the souvenir shop across from your father's office." Eva wasn't sure where this conversation would go but she needed to get the air cleared about how he left her years ago.

"So you never left the reservation?" Billy replied.

"Oh I left. Got my degree in nursing from Oklahoma State. I came back home because I felt an obligation to our people…to help the children if possible. I work part-time at the Clinic and volunteer when I can at the church."

Billy was impressed. "And the souvenir shop….is that yours?"

"Yes, I purchased the shop with the money my father left me when he passed. Everyone said it was a good deal and it is making a small profit, although running the shop keeps me from travelling which I have always wanted to do. It's a big world, Billy and I want to see as much of it as I can someday."

Billy smiled. "Trust me Eva. I've seen a lot of it and most of what I've seen I would just as soon forget. I hope you get your wish, though. It would be more fun to do it with someone but I see no ring on your finger. How did you manage to fight off all the men in your life?"

Eva looked down and just shook her head. "The only man I wanted left me and went off to war." She turned and walked back inside the house without another look at Billy.

CHAPTER 5

Billy attended the investor meeting as invited but chose to be a silent observer rather than jump in to the discussion. Although his father chaired the meeting, one voice in particular drew the most attention and respect…venture capitalist Vincent Califano, a billionaire with reported links to organized crime. Califano was very soft spoken, choosing his words carefully as he asked precise questions about the project he was being invited to invest in.

"So let me be sure I understand this. Your two tribes have selected a site for the casino on the Fort Mohave tribe's land. Is that correct?" Califano was genuinely interested and knew the family would appreciate having an investment the feds could not scrutinize. If it was a tribal property, the government was not allowed to interfere.

Wilson nodded. "Yes, it is a perfect site on the Nevada, Arizona and Colorado border. We have to close on the necessary permits and licenses by the end of the month. We estimate the total cost of the project will approach $65 million, give or take. We have completed the application for a gaming license but the process is much slower than we would like."

After another hour of questions by the entire group, the meeting ended with various commitments to study the proposal with a funding decision within a week. As the group filed out, Califano hung back and asked to speak privately with Wilson. Billy stayed as well at his father's request.

"OK Chief, I like what I see. I think I can convince my group to totally fund the money you need. I can also get the gaming license expedited for you. We want 51% ownership. Simple don't you agree?" Califano knew $65 million was a big nut to swallow, even for the mob family he represented but he didn't see any way the other investors that attended the meeting could come up with anything close to that amount.

Billy had heard enough. "Unacceptable. Without the tribe, this never flies. I think we can find other options. Don't you agree father?"

Wilson was startled by his son's jumping in and he needed time to discuss this offer in private with not only Billy, but the other tribe in Nevada. "Please excuse my son's enthusiasm. You have made a generous and unexpected offer and I need time to discuss it with the council. I will get back to you very soon."

Califano gave Billy a look he had seen many times before from men who wanted to hurt him but ended up getting hurt instead. "Don't wait too long Chief," was the warning.

Califano's driver opened the Escalade's door and they drove off to the Tulsa airport as Billy watched with his father, waiting for the elder to chew him out. "Sorry pop but the man was being totally unreasonable. He thinks we are a bunch of redskins waiting for a handout of fire water."

Father and son walked back to his office in silence. Once inside, Wilson spoke. "Billy, we did our homework on Califano and we know he is part of a notorious mob family looking for safe places to stash their dirty money. Still, he has come to the table with an offer we won't be able to find from a single source, let alone a group with that much liquidity. You are right…51% is not acceptable but we may want to negotiate and see where it gets us."

Billy shook his head in disbelief. "Father I know this type better than you. Even if you negotiate down on their piece, you can't trust them and, in time, they will muscle their way to total control and we end up with nothing but broken jaws. I suggest we wait and see what the rest of the investors come up with. If that doesn't work, we will still have Califano's offer in our pocket."

Wilson saw wisdom in his son's words. "Yes, you make a good point however we are running out of time. We must resolve this by the end of the month or risk the chance that the Fort Mohave Tribe will seek outside money. I would like you to stay a while longer until we wrap this up. Is that a problem?"

Billy's band was scheduled to start a booking at the Stardust Lounge on Monday, three days from today. This was a big opportunity for the band and especially for Billy. Some of the biggest acts in Vegas got their shot at this venue and he could not leave the guys hanging without their lead guitarist.

"Pop, I wish I could but I have a commitment in Vegas with my band. I can't leave them hanging on such short notice." His father never asked him for anything since he returned from Nam and Billy could see the disappointment in his face.

"As you wish," came the answer. "Perhaps you could at least sleep on it. Your people need you, your real people."

Billy agreed. "OK. I'll see you back at the house in a few." He left the council offices and walked across the street to the souvenir shop, hoping to catch Eva before she closed for the evening.

"Hey there Billy Whitehorse. I was just getting ready to close." Eva looked surprised to see him after their last conversation. "When are you leaving town?"

"Tomorrow," Billy replied. "My band is starting a gig at the Stardust next weekend and we need a few days to rehearse and develop our set lists."

"Sounds exciting. Well break a leg or whatever they say to you performers for good luck." Billy could not see the tears in her eyes as she busied herself tidying up the store. She put the "Closed" sign on the door, expecting Billy to leave…but he didn't.

Billy had never gotten over her and his natural impulse was to take her in his arms and kiss her…and he did. Instead of pushing him away, Eva responded with a passion she hadn't felt for years. It was always him in her heart and now he she was in his arms once again.

Without breaking their clenched arms, the couple maneuvered to the back room where they completed their reunion in the most intimate of ways. For Eva, he was the only lover she had ever had. For Billy, she was the only lover he ever cared about.

When they left the shop, the sun had gone down and a breeze had kicked up. They sat on the steps and Billy had a cigarette as Eva stared at the descending darkness of the evening. She knew that what they had enjoyed moments ago was probably a mistake but she didn't want this to end. "Can't you stay a while longer?"

Billy was having the same feelings. "Come with me Eva. You've been stuck here far too long. Let your hair down and have some fun with me for a few days. You owe it to yourself. I promised my father I would come back to help him once this new gig is over or I can find someone to sit in for me."

Eva was almost convinced but she too had obligations and people who depended on her and just throwing caution to the wind for a guy who broke her heart once was too much of a risk. "It's tempting Billy and if I didn't have my own obligations here I would jump at the offer. Besides, if I stay here you have an additional reason to come back."

"You're right," Billy answered. "I'm being selfish I guess but I don't want to lose you again. Give me a week and I'll be back. Believe me."

The next morning over breakfast Billy told his father of his decision. "Give me a week, Pop. I'll find someone to fill in for me and I'll be back. I promise."

Billy then got his things and headed back to the Tulsa airport then back to Vegas.

He found his car right where he parked it and headed back to his apartment. The heat was almost unbearable but nothing he hadn't learned to live with. On the trip back to Vegas, all Billy could think about was Eva. As much as he wanted to be with her, he could not see himself living his days on the reservation doing some meaningless farm work or something even more mundane. That would mean Eva would have to come to him if they were to be together for the long haul.

First order of business was to get his gear over to the Stardust for the new gig tomorrow night. He would tell Willy of the need for a sub when he saw him in person. He stuffed his amp and effects in the back of the Trans Am, keeping his treasured Les Paul up front to avoid any chance of damage on the short drive down the strip.

As usual, he had to lug the gear himself, no roadies for a bar band, he thought as he rolled the Marshall half-stack across the casino floor to the lounge and on to the stage. The rest of the band had already set up and done a preliminary sound check so Billy would have to wing it with the acoustics once the first set started.

Back at his apartment he decided to call Eva, if for no other reason than to hear her voice. He called her house but no one answered. He then called the shop and was told that she hadn't come in yet and probably was at the hospital, her volunteer job when time permitted. He left a message for her and hoped she would call him back that evening.

His next call was to the local Musician's Union to see who might be available to fill in for him. He had developed a good relationship with Byron Taylor, the union rep for Vegas and Byron gave him a list of four guitar players that were available for the following week. They all lived in town and had experience doing studio work and playing for the touring acts who used local musicians.

Billy went down the list and did a mental audition of each player. He knew them all but only one was experienced playing the music that was needed. The others were all very talented but too conservative in their styles for a show band. He made the call and, after giving the details, his replacement was on board. Billy had the new set list and read it to him on the phone. "No problem, brother," came the reply. "I can play those tunes with my eyes closed. Can I use your gear?"

"Sure, no problem except I'm sure you will want to bring your own axe. My Marshall sounds good no matter what goes into it." Billy had no intention of offering his Les Paul but knew any guitarist would prefer using his own instrument at all times.

Billy stopped for a burger and fries at the McDonald's drive-through and returned to his apartment in hopes of getting the return call from Eva. As he ate, he considered the offer made by Vincent Califano. How in the world did his father find this guy, he wondered? Although he was known as a billionaire, there were nothing but unfounded rumors as to how he acquired his fortune. It would take a team of lawyers and CPAs to unravel his network of holdings so the assumed links to organized crimes would be impossible to prove. There had to be a better and less risky alternative for the tribe to finance their project.

As he took the last sip of his drink, the phone rang. It was Eva and she sounded good. "I was hoping you would call," she said. "Sorry I was out. It's been a busy day."

"I can't stop thinking about you Eva. I need you back in my life if you will have me. I will be home in a few days. I found a replacement for the Stardust gig but I need a day or two to get him up to speed before I go."

"I'll be here Billy like I always have."

CHAPTER 6

"Yes the meeting went well Sal. There were other investors there but just minor players. No one can match the deal I offered them." Everyone has bosses, Vincent thought as he gave his report to the head of the syndicate he was representing in his discussions with the tribal leaders. "I think the old chief will roll over but his son is a wild card we may have to deal with."

Salvatore Bellante was not the man his father was. Where the senior was wise and patient, the son was brash and impulsive. Both made the family a shit-load of money but it was a lot more difficult for Sal to keep the appearance of legitimacy in the deals he had put together. Not like the old days where you cracked a few skulls and planted your enemies in the foundation of a building.

"Listen to me Vinnie. We need this to move forward quickly. Having a place on land the feds can't touch will make us millions and gives us the best way to launder our cash from our other operations. This deal was made in heaven." Sal was showing his best attempt at self-control to his partner, but the tension came through none the less. "So what's the deal on the Whitehorse son?"

"He's some war hero from Vietnam. He left the reservation to play music. He is in a Vegas band now but his father places a high value on his opinions so he could end up being a serious problem. How do you want to handle this?" Califano wanted no part of the decision if it involved violence.

"Just sit tight for now," Sal instructed. "If they take our deal then this issue disappears. How much time did you give them to make a decision?"

"He said he had to talk to the other elders. My guess is they need to quit fucking around pretty damn soon."

Sal was finished with the conversation. "OK, follow up with them in a week and press hard for an answer…but be nice. Capisce?"

* * *

The first night at the Stardust went without a hitch. The substitute guitar player sat in and contributed where he could once he got comfortable. After they finished the last set Billy said goodbye and that he would be back in a week. Deville was not happy but there was nothing he could do and the replacement guitar player was decent enough to not cost the band the gig.

Back at his apartment Billy called Eva even though the hour was late. "Eva, good news. I am taking a flight back to Tulsa tomorrow. Tell my dad for me, OK?"

"Billy it's after midnight but I'm glad you called. I'll let your folks know. Call me when you land and I'll pick you up." Eva was delighted that Billy was keeping his word but nothing was ever completely as she hoped and she was prepared for another disappointment…but not for a while.

Not knowing how long he would be gone, Billy took a taxi to the airport and boarded his flight to Tulsa. The plane was almost empty and he had plenty of solitude to think about his future. He loved his music but it was terribly lonely for him in Vegas and now, rediscovering Eva was pulling him back to his roots.

He found the matter of the tribe's casino investment very troublesome, only because of the Califano connection to organized crime. His father was well educated and had incredible connections within the government but was not prepared for the shit storm that was on the horizon if they hooked up with Califano.

Billy's flight arrived on schedule and he called Eva for a ride as she had instructed. In less than an hour, her old F-150 rolled up and they headed back to her place for a passionate reunion they had both been waiting for.

As they lay exhausted from the love making, Eva asked what he expected out of the relationship, almost afraid to hear the answer.

"Eva, I want you in my life. I will never leave you again but I can't guaranty what the future holds for us. I just can't picture a life on the reservation. I've seen too much in too many places to set up my teepee and get fat watching our kids grow up. You need to think this through. I will never expect you to follow me on my journey unless you want it as much as I do."

Eva completely understood. "One day at a time Billy, one day at a time."

Billy met with his father again the following morning, hoping that they had found other investors besides Califano. "Glad you are back, son. Needless to say, we've been busy seeking the funding we need but even with the land locked up, we still haven't been able to put together a package to cover the construction costs. I'm afraid the Fort Mojave Tribe will look for another partner if we fall short. Califano's offer is starting to look like our best and only option."

"Have you said anything to him yet? Let me talk to him man to man…face to face. I'm pretty good at this kind of negotiation so, with luck, he may soften his position."

"Suit yourself son but we are running out of time, like I said." Wilson wrote Califano's direct number for Billy. "The area code is 313. I think it's Detroit."

"OK, I'll give him a call. Tell mother I will be staying at Eva's this trip."

The following morning Eva left for work at the shop she owned. "I'll meet you for lunch," Billy shouted as the pickup backed on to the street.

Billy had a third cup of coffee and another Marlboro before placing the call to Califano. He was amazed that the man actually answered the phone himself.

"Mister Califano, this is Billy Whitehorse. If you have a minute I would like to discuss arranging a meeting."

Califano was equally surprised to be getting this call. "Hey Billy. I thought I would be hearing from your father but go ahead, tell me what's on your mind."

Billy cut right to the chase. "I want to sit down with you and see if we can work out a compromise that can get this project moving forward. I would be happy to come to your office at any time that is convenient."

"No disrespect, Billy but I only negotiate with the actual decision makers…not a surrogate. Let your father know, OK?"

"None taken," Billy answered. "Perhaps you don't understand what I'm saying. I speak for the tribe…both tribes. There will be no deal with you unless we come to an agreement…you and I. If that doesn't work for you, fine. We will consider the offer off the table. Have a nice day." Billy waited a fraction of a second before hanging up and Califano took the bait.

"Hold on, kid. Not so fast. OK, now I get it. Sure, come on in and we can have a pow-wow if that's what you want." He knew the insult would not be overlooked but didn't really give a shit. "Call me back when you have your flight arrangements and I'll have someone meet your plane and drive you to my office."

So Billy would be taking a road trip to Detroit. He hoped the council would cover his ticket and expenses, but the meeting was possibly to determine the financial future of the Cherokees of the Red Bison Clan.

Right at noon, Eva came back to pick up Billy for a quick lunch. "Do you mind if I invite my father? I have important news to go over with him." She agreed and he called his father, deciding they would meet at the Mystic River Diner, a short walk from the Tribal Headquarters.

When they arrived, Wilson was already seated and inspecting the menu. "Welcome back to town, son. And hello again to you Eva. You seem to bring the best out of this warrior I have for a son."

After they placed their orders, Wilson spoke first. "Take a long look at the art on the walls of this place. That picture is of the great chief Sassacus of the Pequot Tribe back in the early 17th century. The one next to him is Captain John Mason, leader of the English troops that killed over 400 of our people at the Mystic River, hence the name of this diner. When you have time you should read up on the history of the Pequots. They are a proud people with a heritage we could all emulate."

They all dug into their meals without further comments until the last bit of gravy was wiped off Billy's plate. "I almost forgot how good the food was in this place. Hell of a lot better than the slop they serve in the Vegas buffet lines."

"Glad you enjoyed the food. Now, any progress in discussions with Califano?" Wilson was watching the clock tick and feared the worst.

"I was able to reach him and he agreed to a sit down at his office in Detroit. I will book my flight today. How tough do you want me to get with this guy? I'm thinking giving them one third ownership is a good starting point."

"They will never accept that offer, Billy. I believe anything less than a controlling interest can work for us, but do your best. A lot is riding on this meeting, son."

Eva dropped Billy back at her place and he called the airlines and made a reservation for his flight to Detroit the following afternoon. After calling Califano's secretary with his flight information, Billy began making notes on what his agenda would be. It was not going to go well, he feared.

CHAPTER 7

The Fort Mohave Indian Reservation spanned 42,000 acres, with almost 6,000 acres located in Clark County Nevada. The Tribal Headquarters was in Needles, California, one of the hottest places in the country with temperatures well into the 100's for weeks at a time.

The Tribal Council Chairman was Shan Williams, a rather young leader whose vision for his tribe was dynamic and well supported. His first major accomplishment was the construction of a PGA Championship Golf Course along the Colorado river, on land that included the new casino site. Revenues were strong and helped fund the Fort Mohave Health Center.

When Damon's call came in Williams was not aware of who was calling nor why. "This is Shan. How can I help you?"

Damon didn't waste time on courtesies. "My name is Damon Drummond. You may have heard of my company, Drummond Construction. We have erected some of the most iconic structures across the country, including the new Drummond Palace in Laughlin.

"Sorry Damon but I never heard of you. Congratulations on your new casino. It is very impressive.

So, what did you want to discuss with me?" Shan knew that the new Drummond casino was having growing pains.

Damon was only slightly embarrassed. "Well let me give you a quick introduction. I have taken the company in a new direction and my first priority was constructing a world class casino resort in Laughlin. Everyone agrees the Palace is a spectacular resort…finer than anything being built in Vegas. Shan laughed. "Well Mr. Drummond, I'm happy for you but what does this have to do with my tribe?"

"I know you are planning to build a casino that will be a direct competitor of the Palace. I think you are making a huge mistake if you go forward with this."

Damon heard the line click off. "You little piece of shit!" he screamed into the phone. He was not going to take a no without a fight. He called down to the valet stand. "This is Mr. Drummond. Please have my car brought to the lobby entrance immediately." Time for a road trip to Needles.

* * *

Billy was able to book a seat on the only non-stop to Detroit, a Delta flight that would take about 2 ½ hours in good weather. Unfortunately, the weather was anything but good in Detroit when he landed…over an hour late. It was a nasty storm…rain turning to sleet turning to snow and the baggage claim area was crowded with people waiting for rides that had come and gone. Billy was one of those.

Califano's limo waited for thirty minutes then left, leaving Billy to his own devices. The driver was kind enough to leave a message for Mister Whitehorse instructing him to take the hotel shuttle to the Ramada where they had booked him a room for the night. Billy assumed they would get to him later for details on his ride to the inner city the next day.

The pickup area for the many airport shuttles was a lengthy walk from baggage claim and open to the elements. Billy was not prepared for a thirty-minute wait with the bitter cold and sleet pelting his thin jacket. Oklahoma had some pretty tough winters but Billy was never as cold as he was that evening.

At last his shuttle appeared and he was welcomed by the blast of a laboring heater that began to finally thaw him out. The drive to the hotel was short and the sleet and darkness hid the scenery that was an indication of the declining state of the once proud motor city.

The hotel was over-booked and the check in line was not moving quickly enough to suit Billy. He decided to head to the bar and kill some time. Beats standing with a line of people pissed and pushy.

The bar had the usual suspects…salesmen on the road looking for companionship. It didn't take long for a long-legged professional to cozy up to Billy at the bar, eager to start a conversation that, if they got lucky, would lead to a quick $50 trick in his room.

Billy's size and appearance usually kept the local bar queens and kings at bay. He was a big, thick man and the long ponytail sent a signal that was fierce and foreboding. It wasn't until they got close that they might guess he was a native American, and sometimes, if the whisky talk turned dark, it was usually too late to keep from feeling his fist in a soft belly.

The girl who took the seat next to Billy was not a typical hooker. She was young, too young in Billy's opinion, and sat for a good ten minutes before turning to Billy for a light. "Got a light?" she asked in a voice that was smoky and soft.

Billy pulled out a Marlboro and lit her cigarette and then his own. "You old enough to drink little girl?" he asked as she released a long stream of smoke into his face.

"Really? You think this place would risk their license serving a minor?" she never really answered his question and Billy let it go.

"Give her another of whatever she's been drinking," Billy instructed the bartender who placed a champagne flute on the bar and filled it with what Billy assumed was alcoholic in nature.

"Thanks. My name is Karen. What's yours?"

"Billy," he answered, now taking in the full picture of the girl in front of him. Tall…probably 5'8; thin…no more than 100 pounds and far too much makeup. She likely painted herself up to disguise her youth which, up close, was all too apparent. His guess was she was no older than 19 and had a pimp nearby to supervise collections.

After taking a sip of her drink, she leaned forward and whispered in Billy's ear. "Are you staying here? I'd love for you to show me your room."

Billy was expecting this. "Sorry young lady but I haven't checked in yet and I'm not really interested in getting arrested for sex with a minor. If you want me to buy you a decent meal, then sit tight and I'll be back after I check in." He got up from his stool and walked over to the check-in desk, never looking back to see if she was leaving.

He got his room key and headed to the elevators and a quick ride to the third floor. His room had two single beds and a small coffee maker for a morning brew. The television was limited to local network channels and there was an ancient clock radio on the night stand. Pretty Spartan accommodations but you get what you pay for. He pulled down the covers and inspected the sheets which appeared to be clean, at least to the naked eye.

Billy splashed some water on his face and inspected his appearance. The scars of combat were hidden for the most part and he looked presentable enough for a young hooker eager to get a meal into her belly. He left his packed bag on the bed and headed back to the elevators.

When Billy walked back to the bar he found Karen had a friend standing next to her…a tall skinny black man trying his best Superfly impersonation but he didn't have the physical tools to back up the bad ass look. Billy guessed he had a weapon in the man-purse slung over his shoulder. They don't make pimps like they did in Saigon.

"Is this your new friend baby?" the pimp asked as Billy walked up.

Billy ignored the man and the comment. "You ready to grab a bite Karen?" The young girl was frozen in fear…waiting for her pimp to answer. Instead, the pimp stood nose to nose with Billy.

"You gots to pay to play brother. And I ain't talking about a burger and fries. This little lady will ride you like a rollercoaster, so let's cut all the bullshit and get down to business."

Billy took a quick scan of the bar, making sure his back was to the room, then grabbed the pimp by his balls, squeezing as hard as he could. Without releasing his grip, he slowly lowered the pimp to the floor, covering his painful scream with his free hand.

Billy could see the man's eyes rolling back and released his grip a moment before he passed out from the pain. Karen was crying, knowing the outcome for her would not be good. The bartender saw the whole thing but acted like nothing had happened.

"Looks like my friend has had one too many," Billy announced to anyone who could hear. He lifted the pimp to his feet and walked him to a nearby booth, taking a seat across from him.

"I don't know your name and really don't give a shit how you make a living," Billy whispered, but loud enough to be certain his words were heard and understood. "Unless it involves underage girls like Karen, so listen carefully. Karen and I are going to walk across the lobby to the restaurant and have a nice dinner. When we are finished eating we will come back to this bar. You will not be there. If you are, I will put you in the hospital. Just nod your head that you understand what I just said." The pimp nodded.

"Now hand me that silly fucking purse you are carrying." The pimp handed it across the table and Billy inspected the contents. There was a chrome plated .38 Smith & Wesson, a wallet, spiral notebook, car keys, and a wad of cash with a rubber band around it. Billy slipped the gun under his shirt and handed the cash to Karen.

"That's a lot of fucking money you got there," the pimp mumbled. "A lot of people are going to be very upset if that disappears. You might want to reconsider. Ain't no bitch worth the ass-whipping you gonna end up with if you keep fucking with me." Obviously his bravado increased as the pain in his groin subsided.

Billy took Karen's arm and they slid out of the booth. "Have a nice day cocksucker," Billy said as they left the bar.

In the lobby, Billy led the girl to the gift shop instead of the restaurant. "I want you to take this money and get to the airport right away. If you stick around that prick will kill you. Where are you from?"

"My folks live in Chicago. I ran away about a year ago and took the bus here. Sugar saw me at the bus station and offered to help me get settled. I think you can guess the rest of the story."

Billy took the roll of cash and gave a quick count. "Looks like you have around $5,000 here Karen. Enough to get you a plane ticket home or wherever you choose. The bottom line is you can't stay here. Do you understand?"

While Billy was talking, she could see the pimp run out of the bar and to the parking lot. "He just left. When he comes back he won't be alone mister. I don't why you got involved but I'm really not worth it."

"Enough. We don't have much time. Stay here while I get you a cab."

Billy went to the valet desk and, as luck would have it, a cab had just rolled up to let off a customer. "Hold on," Billy yelled and ran and got Karen.

Karen looked at the open door of the waiting taxi and turned to Billy. She wrapped her thin arms around him and gently kissed his mouth. No words were said or needed.

As the cab sped off into the night Billy wondered where she would end up. He guessed it was 50-50 that she would be sitting in that same bar in a few days…if she was still alive.

CHAPTER 8

Billy knew that helping the young hooker was a huge mistake. It was more than a distraction from his mission. It could likely get his ass in the hospital or in the ground. No point in staying at the Ramada now. He would need to find another place to spend the night. He quickly went back to his room to retrieve his bag and took the stairs back to the lobby, carefully looking to see if the bad guys had arrived. So far so good, he thought to himself.

He put his light jacket on and walked through the lobby and out the front door, just as a gold El Dorado pulled in to the parking lot. The four men jumped out of the large Cadillac and the pelting sleet made it impossible for them to see Billy standing in the shadows. He watched as they stormed in to the hotel, hands hidden from view. Billy calculated it would take at least ten minutes for them to discover he was not in his room and another fifteen minutes for them to sweep the bar and restaurant. He had enough time to get to the Holiday Inn about two hundred yards further down the road.

By the time Billy reached the Holiday Inn he was coated with frozen rain, almost looking like a living snowman. No one was manning the check-in desk and

Billy took the time he had to wait to defrost and regain feeling in his hands and face.

Finally a young kid in a green vest much too large for him came to check in his new guest. Probably a local college student working during Christmas break, Billy assumed as he placed the credit card from the Tribe on the counter. "Need a room for the night," Billy announced.

"Did you make a reservation?" the kid asked per the usual routine.

"No I didn't."

"Well I think we can handle this. We have a room with two double beds. Will that work for you? You also get a complimentary continental breakfast. Just hand the voucher to the waitress in the restaurant."

"Perfect," Billy answered and headed to his room on the seventh floor. As he exited the elevator he saw an area with an icemaker and vending machine. He fed the appropriate amount of coins into the machine and grabbed a coke and small bag of pretzels...his feast for the evening.

Billy fell on to the much too soft bed and fell asleep instantly...fully clothed.

Billy's internal clock woke him up precisely at five o'clock. It was two a.m. Vegas time...when he would normally be finishing a gig and heading to one of the endless buffets that served food 24/7.

He looked out his window into the dark morning sky and was pleased that the shitty weather had ended. He could handle the cold if it was accompanied by a sunny blue sky. First order of business was to see if Califano had left him a message at the Ramada where Billy had checked in and, officially, was still there.

The front desk at the Ramada was busy with check-outs when Billy called. "Mister Whitehorse, we've been ringing your room all morning. You have quite a fan club. The night manager said a group of men stormed around wanting to know where you were last night."

"That's great but were there any messages left for me this morning?"

"Yes, a Mister Califano called twice this morning. He left his number for you to call him back. He said it was urgent."

Billy took down the number and told the manager he would not be returning and to go ahead and bill his credit card for the room charge.

After a much needed cup of coffee Billy dialed the number and was surprised to hear Califano answering. "Where in the fuck have you been?"

"Sorry, I had a situation I had to deal with and I had to move to another hotel. I hope our meeting is still on."

"Sure, it's still on but you have to find your own transportation to my office. I don't have anyone available to pick you up. Get to the Renaissance Center and find the Northwest Tower…the 200 Tower. My offices are on the 37th floor. Any cab driver will know exactly where it's at. Hurry. I don't have all fucking day."

Billy memorized the directions and called down to the lobby to order a cab for him in one hour. He needed to try out the free breakfast before he left for the meeting. As he ate his yogurt and Danish he wondered where Karen spent the night. Hopefully on an airplane to Chicago. He knew he would wonder about the young girl for a long time and if he could have done more.

The cab arrived around 10:30 and Billy gave the driver the address. "This your first visit to the Ren Cen?" the driver asked. "Got some fine shops and restaurants. Designer shit like Dior, Channel, Ralph Lauren. Mayor is hoping it turns the city around. GM and Ford are moving in to two of the office towers." He kept talking as he drove, giving Billy a guided tour of the inner city that once was the diamond of US manufacturing. "You want I'll swing by Motown's headquarters. They still making hits in that little place. Not the best part of town though."

In twenty minutes, they were on West Jefferson Avenue and Billy was blown away by the 70-story structure towering over the river front. "Damn that is one tall building."

"The tall one in the middle is the hotel. Hell of a restaurant on the top of it. The smaller towers around it are all offices." A few minutes later the cab pulled up at the main entrance of the Detroit Plaza Hotel. "Here you go buddy. Good luck finding the tower you want. It's like a maze in there. First timers always get lost."

Billy jumped out, paid the cabbie and asked the bellman how to get to Tower 200. He was directed through the hotel lobby to the main courtyard which was connected by escalators going every which way and up to levels of shops that were also connected to the elevator banks for each tower. Man I could spend a day in this place and still get lost…and he did.

After asking several people moving quickly with brief cases in tow, he finally found the right tower and took the ride to the 37th floor which appeared to be totally occupied by Califano and Company. The glass entry doors were locked and required a pass key to get in. There was a telephone on the wall to get passage for visitors which Billy used, announcing he was there for a meeting with Vincent Califano. No one answered but the doors buzzed open and he entered.

The floor was a mass of cubicles in a circle with the executive offices on the outer wall…all with spectacular views of the Detroit River and Canada. In the center was a large reception area with several secretary types buzzing around doing what secretaries do. Billy walked up and got the attention of one girl, in her early 20's he guessed, and announced who he was and why he was there.

"Please have a seat Mister Whitehorn and I'll let Mister Califano know you are here."

"Whitehorse…my name is Whitehorse…not Whitehorn." Billy announced and took a seat in a very expensive chrome and leather chair with a glass table next to it with the latest magazines in a neat stack to choose from.

As he sat, flipping through the latest Forbes, he took in the general atmosphere of the place. Men, mostly just out of college, were walking back and forth carrying file folders and leather portfolios with the Califano name embossed in the cover. All had formal office attire…dress shirts and pants and wide colorful ties which were very much in style. A few had facial hair and side burns that were long but again, in style. The girls, which seemed to outnumber the guys by a lot, wore skirts and dresses…no pants that Billy could see. There were a lot of trees and plants all over the floor and Billy guessed they were not fake, requiring regular care by an outside service. All in all, a pleasant atmosphere to earn a living in.

Thirty minutes passed and Billy was getting antsy. He wasn't used to sitting in one place for such a long period. He needed to move around…get the blood flowing in his legs. "Excuse me. Could you tell me where the rest-room is?" The girl who directed him to his seat sent him down a hallway where he found the Men's room. When he returned to his waiting spot another young girl, much prettier than the last one, was waiting for him.

"Mr. Whitehorse, please follow me," she instructed and led him to what appeared to be the executive suites, separated by another glass security door from the main working areas. She slid her pass card through the magnetic reader and the doors opened. She led him to the farthest corner where the big man's office was located. She knocked twice then opened the door and Billy walked in where Califano was on the phone, never looking up to see his new visitor.

The doors closed behind him and he was alone and took a seat in front of Califano's spacious desk. A minute later the call ended and Califano spun around in his chair to face Billy. "Well finally. Guess things move slower on the reservation than they do here. So, do we have a deal or not?"

Billy locked eyes with Califano. "We do not, but I am here to see if we can work things out so that we do have a deal."

"I'm listening," came the reply.

Billy pulled a contract he had prepared from his jacket but simply laid it on the table, not saying a word about its contents. "We agree that the total cost of the construction will come in around $60 million of which you have offered to cover the entire amount. For that you want controlling interest which, as I'm sure you already know, is illegal for a tribal enterprise. Controlling ownership must be in the name of the tribe."

Califano didn't blink. "We can work around that. Trust me. We have friends in high places."

"I'm sure you do but that is irrelevant. There is no way in hell you will have financial control. What I can do is this. We will give you 40% for an investment of $40 million. You will secure the necessary license with the gaming commission. We will provide the land and the remaining funds from other sources. In addition, we will give you 51% ownership of the marina and golf course. We calculate that to be worth a significant amount to you, long term…potentially equal to what the remaining 11% ownership would have provided. It's all spelled out in this contract I brought. Sign it and we have a deal."

Califano picked up the contract and flipped through its pages, then threw it back at Billy. "Fuck you. We dictate terms not you and 40% is not gonna cut it." This bravado was all for show as the deal was not half bad. He needed to bounce it off Bellante. "Now get the fuck out of here. If we change our mind on your offer, you'll hear from me but don't hold your breath."

Billy stood and smiled as he left. Califano kept the contract. He was interested.

CHAPTER 9

Elena was seeing a side of her lover that surprised and frightened her. Damon was abrupt and intolerant when she offered an opinion and rarely called when he was going to be late or out of town. Her hours as a dancer kept them from spending much time with each other which was probably for the best given the tension growing between them. Still, she needed to talk to him about something that could affect the relationship...she was pregnant.

When she called his office to see when he would be home she learned he had taken an unannounced trip by car to Needles. Jill Beauville was not an admirer of Damon but felt sorry for Elena and told her not to worry. He wouldn't be gone long.

* * *

It was a sunny day and hot as hell. Damon toyed with the thought of putting the top down on his SL but knew it would be a lot hotter crossing the desert and just turned up the AC and slipped a Fleetwood Mac cassette into his car radio.

Traffic was light and as he entered reservation land he knew he was ceding his rights to those of the tribal police and court system. One hundred years earlier he would have been putting his life in danger testing the patience of the people who came before us. He would be on his best behavior.

As he drove down US40, he exited on Historic Route 66, then north on to O Street. Five blocks later he was at the Tribal Headquarters on Merriman Street…a stone's throw from the Colorado River which was the official border with Arizona. The building looked as though it was a new construction…very modern with lots of glass and marble. He was impressed.

There was no formal parking lot so Damon parked the Mercedes at the curb in front of the building. He checked to be sure there were no parking restrictions posted. The last thing he needed was getting his car impounded on an Indian reservation.

He climbed the short flight of steps to the entrance and was greeted by a dark-skinned woman wearing traditional garments of her tribe. On the table surrounding her were numerous books and artifacts about the tribe's culture and heritage. Some were free but most were for sale. "How can I help you?" she asked.

"I'd like to see Shan Williams. Is he in?"

"I'm sorry, Shan is at lunch. Did you have an appointment?"

"I spoke to him the other day. I'm just following up on that conversation. I drove in from Las Vegas."

"Well you are welcome to take a seat and wait for him. We have some interesting reading materials about our people if you are interested."

"Do you have any idea where he might be having lunch? Maybe I could talk to him while he eats." Damon was impatient by nature and had no desire to cool his heels reading tribal propaganda.

"You might try Cooks Cuisine. It's just a few blocks from here on Needles Highway and Race Street. If he gets back before you see him, I'll let him know you were here."

Damon left without thanking the lady and fired up his car, noting how hot the leather seats had become. "Need some fucking sheep skins," he mumbled to himself and waited for the A/C to cool down the interior a minute before proceeding.

He had no difficulty finding the restaurant which was filled with natives enjoying a break from the heat. He had no idea what Shan looked like so he asked a waitress if he was there and she pointed to a corner booth with four men finishing their meals.

Damon approached the booth and, as he walked through the diner, every head turned and watched him. With his long blonde hair, he must have looked like Custer at the Little Big Horn. "Excuse me fellas. Which of you is Shan Williams? My name is Damon Drummond."

The three that were dining with Shan quickly excused themselves, leaving only one man in the booth. He was much younger than Damon imagined, maybe late 30's and tall and thin. Damon was 6' 2" but no one would accuse him of being thin. Shan was wearing a suede sports coat and denim jeans with a crisp crease in each leg. He had an open collared checkered blue shirt and a stainless Rolex Submariner on his wrist. "Well I must say I'm surprised to see you here Mister Drummond. I thought I was pretty clear in my response to you on the phone."

Damon slid into the vacated space directly in front of Williams. A waitress quickly walked up and Damon ordered an iced tea. "You were pretty abrupt with me on the phone Mr. Williams and I thought I needed to make my case more clearly and in person. Always better in person."

"Well I was just finishing my lunch and I have a full afternoon scheduled so I guess this will have to do. What do I have to do to make you go away Mr. Drummond?"

Drummond was losing his patience. "Listen, I know you need money to get your casino built. I also know you have partnered with another tribe but they are having trouble coming up with the cash. This whole thing is a loser for you guys. I will put you out of business in the first year. Why piss away all that time and money? I can solve your problem. Trash your plan and I'll make it worth your while."

Shan stood up, placed several bills on his ticket and walked away. He had nothing more to say and was making his point the best way he could. He was not the type to argue in public.

"Hold on you little shit. I drove a long way to see you and you better sit your ass down." Damon had raised his voice to the point that the remaining diners heard him loud and clear. Two of the diners stood up and walked slowly towards Damon. They were tribal police officers.

"Is there something you need?" the tallest officer asked. The other had pulled out his night stick and was eager to be given a reason to use it on this big mouth.

"No, no, everything's fine. I was just leaving." Damon cooled down quickly in the face of an ass-whipping that was surely to follow if he continued to be belligerent.

"Good. Have a nice day and be sure to drop by the gift shop for a nice piece of turquoise jewelry for your wife." The officer left barely enough room for Damon to squeeze past him and out the door.

Damon stood by his car and there was no sign of Shan who wasted no time getting back to his office where he instructed his staff that under no circumstance was Damon Drummond to set foot in their building. Then he picked up the phone and called Wilson Whitehorse.

"Wilson, this is Shan. You won't believe what just happened here. The owner of the Palace drove in from Vegas and is trying to muscle us into not going forward with the casino. He called me first and I told him to piss off then he shows up at my door barking orders like he owned the place."

"What is his name?" Wilson asked, wondering if the man had ties to the Califano group.

"His name is Damon Drummond. His father is a well-respected real estate developer out of Dallas. He is the real deal but his kid is a piece of work."

Wilson was relieved that no one from Califano's group was involved although an end run around his tribe was not out of the realm of possibility. He needed to hear from Billy soon as things were beginning to unravel.

CHAPTER 10

Billy wasted no time getting a cab to take him to the airport. He had left his return open when he purchased his ticket and hoped he could get a seat back to Tulsa without much of a delay. The Delta counter was almost empty so his hopes were high. The next non-stop to Tulsa was in three hours and he bought a ticket in spite of the delay.

He decided to grab a bite then call his father with an update on his discussion with Califano. He debated how to frame the meeting. He was confident Califano would take his offer but his father wanted concrete facts, not gut feelings.

"Hey pop, I'm at the airport heading back in a couple of hours."

"How did it go with Califano?" his father was quick to ask.

"He was belligerent and condescending, just like he was when he came to visit us. I must say I was impressed with his office. He must employ at least one hundred people in his headquarters and they all appear to be well-educated and eager to climb the ladder. His company manages a pretty substantial hedge fund, whatever that is. I think he basically takes subscriber money and reinvests in high risk, high return stocks and bonds. My guess is the lions share is mob money that he launders."

"So what did he decide? Will he come down from his initial demand?"

Billy had to be honest with his father. "He said no but I believe he will come around once he talks to his bosses. Trust me on this. I know the type."

"Well we have another problem to deal with. The owner of the Palace paid a call on Shan Williams making threats. Seems like he doesn't want a competitor on his door step. We can talk about this when you get back."

It was almost time to board his flight but he had one more call to make. He dialed the Ramada's number and asked for the bar which was empty. "Is Karen around?" he asked the person who answered.

"No. Too early for her. No customers yet. Who is this?"

"Just a friend," Billy answered. "Just a friend."

* * *

As Damon drove home, he considered how far he had come since his father threw the envelope with the million dollars across the table. With the backing of Aubrey Bennison and the assets of Drummond Construction, the Palace was born. It was everything

Damon had dreamed of but much too ostentatious for his father's tastes. Everything was painted, plated or real gold. The rooms rivaled the finest hotels in Vegas and Damon was able to convince some of the high-end designers to open shops on the property. When it opened and for several months after, major entertainers were booked and provided top flight shows for the crowds that flocked to the new landmark. The only thing missing was the Drummond name.

Bennison was adamant about not having the Drummond name on the buildings. He had invested enough that he had veto power and used it. Damon planned on changing the name once he had paid back much of Aubrey's initial funding.

Along the way, Damon added a new wife and child to his life. Elena was now a full time mother to their daughter Nicole. Once the Palace was completed, Damon moved his family and office to the penthouse. It was a short ninety-minute drive from Vegas but far enough that he didn't have Bennison looking over his shoulder.

Unfortunately, the same could not be said about his father who insisted that Jill Beauville join him as the Casino Manager. In preparation for her new role, Jill spent endless hours working behind the scenes at Bennison's properties learning every facet of the gaming business. She became the brains behind the glitter and was constantly reining in Damon from expensive excesses.

Initially Damon threw himself into his new role of husband and father. Although he bragged that he never changed a diaper, Damon made sure he provided important parenting time to little Nicky as he called his daughter.

In time, however, old urges and perversions were creeping back into his personality. With the Palace right under the nose of his wife, he began to take frequent trips to Las Vegas, some overnight. Over the years he had fancied himself to be a playboy with frequent, if not meaningful, dalliances with plenty of ladies…always young and impressionable. Perhaps that was why he was losing interest in Elena. She was still stunningly beautiful and her figure returned quickly after childbirth. But…she was not the youngest filly in the stable.

His latest visit to Vegas was to promote featuring the Miss USA pageant at the Palace. He met with the pageant officials and sponsors and promised an extravaganza worthy of the event. Part of his pitch was the promise of extensive television coverage which, initially, was a brazen lie. He would need Bennison's help to reel in a network to cover the event and that would cost him. With that commitment, the pageant officials signed the contract and a date was chosen in February. Dick Clark was to be the master of ceremonies but Damon intended to be visibly active in all stages of the competition and offered to be one of the judges which he added as a last-minute revision to the final contract. He couldn't wait to see the photos of the girls that would compete for the title.

* * *

During the flight back to Tulsa, Billy could not stop thinking about Karen. He hoped for the best but feared the worst. If he could have stayed, he was certain he could have made sure she got on an airplane and left the shit-hole life she had been leading. In a dark way, she reminded him of the young girls in Saigon that earned their livings satisfying the needs of horny GI's like Billy miles away from home. He promised himself he would reach out to her again.

Eva was waiting for him as he de-planed and was eager to hear the details of his trip. She had read the dark headlines about the inner city of Detroit and worried about Billy's safety every hour he was gone.

"Yes there are some really rough sections but the new Renaissance Center is really turning the inner city around. It is a beautiful structure. Almost like a phoenix rising from the ashes."

"Did your meeting go well? I know your father has been pacing the floor waiting for your return." Eva's relationship with Billy was drawing her in to the family circle and Wilson called her several times in Billy's absence to see if she had heard from him.

"My meeting was productive but nothing has been resolved. Still I'm optimistic so we need to celebrate. What do you say?" Billy wanted to get his mind off of Karen and was eager to dive in to some beers and pizza with the woman he loved.

Billy was still learning to like the food he grew up on but missed the junk food that helped him grow from the skinny farm boy to the hulk of muscle he became in the war. People meeting him for the first time were back on their heels a bit. Add some war paint and he would be the personification of all the Indian warriors seen in low budge westerns.

As they drove east on US44, Billy kept his eyes open for a friendly sign and found an Arby's and Burger King just off 165th Ave. East. They pulled in to the Arby's and went inside rather than use the drive through window. Billy was hungry and piled his tray with roast beef sandwiches and fries. Eva had just a coke and order of fries.

"Hey babe, your making me look like a pig. Have one of my sandwiches." He placed one on her tray but she handed it back to him.

"Thanks but I'm trying to watch what I eat these days."

"Seriously? You are in perfect shape. Trust me I've inspected the goods up close and personal."

Eva smiled but Billy could see she had something on her mind. "Are you feeling OK?" he asked, looking carefully in to her eyes.

"Billy, I missed my last period. I think I'm pregnant. I didn't want to say anything until I was sure. I'm sorry." Eva began to cry and the minute Billy saw the first tear in her eyes he jumped to her side of the booth and wrapped his arms around her.

"You just made me the happiest guy in the world, Eva. I love you.... always have. We will have a wonderful life together. Let's get married right away." Billy had lost his appetite and wanted to tell the good news to everyone he saw.

Eva immediately cheered up and soaked in all the joy Billy was showing. "Are you sure?" she asked him. "Maybe we should wait until I hear back from the doctor."

"Baby or no baby, I want to marry you Eva. I'm tired of being alone. Please say yes."

Eva gave him her answer by smothering him in kisses, oblivious to the other diners. Minutes later they were out the door and heading to tell his parents the good news.

CHAPTER 11

"It's not a bad deal, Sal. I've run the numbers and it gets our feet in the door without any muscle. That can come later." It was always easier to talk to Bellante face to face. On the phone he was a ball breaker but across a table he showed considerable restraint…up to a point.

"It's the fucking kid. He's the one with the *cagliones*, not his father. Take the kid out of the equation and the old man rolls over. Done and done. Make it happen."

"You want to kill the Whitehorse son? You're getting way ahead of this Sal. If we take baby steps, we win it all without bringing any heat down on us. Those Indian cops are not playing by the rules we're used to. If we fuck with one of theirs we may all end up buried in the desert." Califano had never tested his boss like this before and was crossing a line one never crossed.

Sal stood and walked to the credenza where the liquor bottles sat. He poured three fingers of Scotch and walked back to his seat. "Vincent, I love you like a brother and appreciate your consul but on this issue there is no compromise. You have your instructions. Now get the fuck out before I slit your throat!"

Califano walked along the river back to his Ren-Cen office. He had just pushed Sal too far and it could ultimately cost him his life. If he sent a crew to Oklahoma they wouldn't get within 100 yards of the reservation before they had major tribal heat on their ass. He had to draw Billy Whitehorse to their turf to have a good chance of taking him out.

"Jennifer, get Wilson Whitehorse on the phone please." The secretary placed the call and Wilson answered almost immediately.

"Mr. Califano, good to hear from you. Billy says you two had a productive meeting. I hope you are calling to say we have a deal."

"Well I'm not sure I would say it was a productive meeting. The contract he offered was not even close to what we could accept. Having said that, the door is still open which is why I'm calling. I want to arrange another meeting with you guys. If you want to send Billy that's fine. My attorney has drafted some ideas that we need to bounce off you. Who knows, you might like what we come up with and we can move forward quickly."

Wilson wished that Billy was with him but he knew he had landed and was heading back shortly. "Thanks for the invitation but I'm not sure we have anything more to offer than what Billy gave you. We have other options that we are reviewing but Billy will be here in an hour and I will talk to him about what you've suggested. We'll get back to you tomorrow."

That evening there was an impromptu celebration at the Whitehorse house over the wedding that would precede the birth of Wilson's first grandchild. Billy and Eva were on top of the world and Eva was careful to steer clear of the "firewater". Billy and the others, on the other hand, got shit-face drunk. The following morning the house was littered with partygoers who crashed where they were sitting when the last bottle was drained.

Wilson hadn't had a chance to discuss Califano's call with Billy and chose to bring it up over breakfast. Billy listened carefully as Wilson went through the conversation in great detail, leaving nothing out. "Before you say anything, son, I need to tell you about another conversation I had the other day with Shan Williams. It seems the owner of the Palace paid a visit to the Fort Mohave Tribe. He expressed his displeasure with our pending project and demanded we back off. I'm sure there is some money he wants to throw at us to make us go away."

"What did Shan tell him?" Billy asked.

"He told him to get lost. I think his exact words were to "fuck off". Billy had never heard his father use the f-bomb and it made him laugh harder than he should have. "Glad you find this so funny."

"So it's back to Detroit. Maybe I'll bring Eva with me. She needs to see life in a big industrial city." Billy was excited to get Eva away from the Reservation and, if the opportunity presented itself, he would check on Karen as well. "Set it up pop. I can go whenever you say."

* * *

Califano hung up the phone after taking Wilson Whitehorse's call. He had three days to set up the hit…barely enough time to get the right assets in place. He decided to put Billy up at the Plaza. It was near the river and he could bring in shooters from Windsor who could get in and out quickly. If all went well, Billy Whitehorse would be sleeping at the bottom of the Detroit River in less than a week. The message to his father would be loud and clear.

The Detroit Partnership was a mafia family that traced its Detroit roots all the way back to the end of the first World War. Through the years it transitioned from one group to another and came to a bloody conclusion in 1919 with the introduction of the Volstead Act. Ongoing turf wars continued for decades until the ascension of Joseph Zerilli.

Joseph "Joe Z." Zerilli was one of the most respected American Mafia bosses of his era. He quietly ruled his crime family and underworld domain as a traditional Mafia boss who would take with him to the grave one of the American underworld's most famous secrets, who killed Teamster Union president Jimmy Hoffa.

Zerilli had a fondness for Sal Bellante and relegated many of the day to day decisions to his younger protégé. This included the respectable arms of the family like Califano's group. When Vincent needed muscle, Sal provided it. Windsor was a different animal. While there was no recognized mob family in control of the Canadian underworld, several gangs sprang up that would contract their skills to the Italians across the river. Califano knew them all and chose the one that had been the most effective and discreet on past assignments.

The Wild Jokers was known as a Windsor biker gang that was ruthless and effective. The truth was that having a motorcycle was not a membership requirement but the iron horse image kept them under the radar of law enforcement focused on organized crime. Their president, Stinky Jordan, was an ex-military policeman and had legendary skills with all types of small arms. His closest henchmen were also former military with extensive combat experience in Southeast Asia and elsewhere.

Califano left a message at the gang's club house and got a return call from Stinky in less than an hour. "Hey little Vinnie…long time no talk. So, you called. I assume you have some work for my guys."

"I do but you have a short window…three days to get it done." Califano went on to describe Billy and provided the details on when he was to arrive and where he would be staying.

"Not a problem but it will cost you. $50,000 sounds like a reasonable number to take out one guy. You good with that?" Stinky would have done it for less but the urgency in Califano's voice implied he would not split hairs on the money involved.

"OK. Come by my office when it's done and pick up the money. One thing you should know. This guy is a bad ass war hero from Vietnam. He looks to be in pretty good shape so take no chances." Stinky laughed at the warning.

"Thanks Vinnie. We'll be real careful."

* * *

"But Billy, I have a business to run and obligations. I can't just walk away for a wild weekend with my fiancé." Eva was putting up a weak fight and Billy knew it. She wanted to make the trip to Detroit and finally agreed that things would not fall apart if she was gone for a couple of days. Billy had his father's complete confidence to act on behalf of the tribe and they concluded that if they gave ground, it would be minimal.

Before boarding their flight to Detroit, Billy checked the weather and was pleased that it would be cold but clear….no rain or snow was forecasted. This trip he made sure to have a warm pea coat for himself and a hooded parka for Eva. The wind was intense as it blew between the tall buildings and the river and they had some walking to do.

Eva was dealing with some mild morning sickness but nothing that would prevent her from flying. They agreed that when they returned she would pick an OBGYN and start on whatever pre-natal protocols that were prescribed. She wanted a boy; he wanted a girl…go figure.

CHAPTER 12

"We're losing our ass Damon…big league!" Jill Beauville was not painting a very rosy picture. "We have to cut back and quickly. The renovations we've started have become a black hole. And the rumors of a new casino popping up in our backyard are not helping…believe me."

Damon saw this coming but his ego told him he could power through it if he stopped paying people…starting with the contractors working on the renovations. Jill fought him on this knowing the long-term blowback that would occur. Once they got a reputation as a dead beat, lenders, of whom there were many, would hunker down.

"No. We go forward on the renovations. They must be completed before the Miss USA Pageant. Just string the contractors out on payments. You know how to do this; lost invoices, pricing errors,"

"Damon…if word gets out about our finances they might move the pageant. This is a no win situation for us. Wake up!" Jill was done fighting with someone with the integrity of a charlatan. Next step was to go to Wilfred and let the chips fall where they may.

Damon needed an infusion of cash but knew the banks carrying his current sizeable debt would never expand their risk on a failing enterprise. He was convinced that hosting Miss USA would generate new momentum for the Palace and bring the high-rollers back. His only viable option was going back to Bennison hat in hand.

"Don't do anything yet." Damon instructed Jill as he left the office for a quick trip to Las Vegas. He knew Aubrey was in town and didn't want to risk being shut down on a phone call.

As Damon drove to confront Bennison, he tried to calculate how much he needed to keep things moving forward. He also knew that if the Indian casino opened he might be forced into bankruptcy, a scenario Bennison was sure to bring up.

* * *

"Mr. Bennison will see you now." The cute receptionist got up to lead Damon but he knew the way and she returned to her desk. He entered the office without knocking and walked immediately to a chair directly in front of Bennison's large antique desk from the late 1700's.

"The size of your ego never ceases to amaze me. If you didn't owe me $10 million I would have your ass thrown out the door." Bennison was not at all happy to see

Damon without an appointment. "What the fuck is so urgent?"

"You know we are working our asses off to get the Palace ready for the Miss USA Pageant in a couple of months. That is sucking up most of our cash flow and I am tapped out on my credit lines with the banks. I need money, Aubrey. Once the pageant is over, the flood gates will open and we will be rolling in clover."

"How much?" Bennison asked without looking up from the papers on his desk.

"Ten million." Damon answered. "That will get all the renovations completed and cover the expenses of the participants and the pageant staff including Dick Clark. who doesn't come cheap."

"How much is your family kicking in?" Now Bennison was looking squarely into Damon's eyes.

"Nothing." Damon answered. "That's why I had to use outside contractors. The family wants no part of the project."

Bennison began to laugh…always a bad sign thought Damon. "You're done kiddo. Not another penny will be coming from me. In fact, when the Miss USA people dump your sorry ass I will have the pageant moved to one of my Vegas casinos. If I were you I would crawl back to Dallas and beg daddy for a job…maybe cleaning the toilets."

"Fuck you!" Damon yelled back. "I'll find the money somewhere else. And if you leak a word of this to the Miss USA people I will sue your fat ass for a hell of a lot more than what I am asking for." Damon stormed out of Bennison's office and stopped in the nearest lounge to regain his composure.

"Give me a double Chivas," he ordered the barmaid. He watched as she poured the 12-year-old scotch over the large ice cubes and saw the marriage of liquor and ice turn into a milky liquid. He tilted his head back and let the drink slide slowly down his throat, creating a slightly bitter taste that was so familiar and comforting.

"What the fuck have I done?" he asked himself as he drained his glass. "Again!" he instructed and finished the second drink without taking a breath. If he filed for bankruptcy, he would at least protect his personal assets and his family would be shielded from recourse. The damage to his reputation would be massive but, in time, he would get another swing of the bat. The damage to the good name of his father, however, would never recover and that was the one thing he was most sensitive to. He had to find another option.

* * *

The drive from Detroit Metro to the Renaissance Center took almost forty-five minutes in traffic and they arrived just as many of the office workers were leaving the towers to catch the Grand Trunk train to the northern suburbs. Billy watched Eva's eyes grow wide as she took in the mammoth structures on the Detroit skyline and Canada just across the river.

A bellman greeted their arrival and promptly gathered up their luggage as they proceeded to the front desk. "It looks like a Christmas postcard Billy. Look at all the shops. I've only seen those brands in magazines."

"I'm sure we'll have enough time to browse through them before we fly back. Maybe we can get you a nice maternity outfit at Chanel." She laughed and gave Billy a soft punch before they entered the elevator.

At the concierge desk a call was being made to Vincent Califano's private line. "He just checked in. Room 2025. He brought a woman with him."

Vinnie was not expecting another person with Billy. If he called Stinky with the news it would surely raise the cost. Best to leave things as they were. If the woman falls so be it.

Again, he had to leave a message at the gang's club house and, as before, it took only a few minutes for Stinky to return the call. "He just checked in. Room 2025. He is going to call me in the morning to set up our meeting. I'll set it up for late lunch at Joe Muer's on the Riverwalk. Make sure he never makes the meeting."

Stinky had picked his two best lieutenants to handle the hit. "OK boys…it's show time. Here's a picture of the guy. It's old but from what I've been told he is in pretty good shape like he was when he got home from Nam. The picture was from a Tulsa newspaper article about the returning war hero. It was good enough. Indians never age, right?"

The shooters would cross the river in the morning by car and get in position before the lunch crowd erupted on to the streets. Billy would have to make the short walk from the hotel down to the Riverwalk where they would arrange a cross fire with silenced Uzi's. Easy peasy. By the time any cops arrived they would be crossing back into Windsor.

"The room is unbelievable Billy. Can we afford this?" Eva walked to the balcony and took in a panoramic view that was truly breathtaking. Billy walked up behind her and gently kissed her neck before lighting a cigarette.

"Califano comped the room this time so let's enjoy his generosity while we can. I made dinner reservations at the Summit on top of the hotel so get ready."

Once they were seated, Billy ordered a bottle of Dom Perignon and, once glasses were filled, he pulled a small box from his coat jacket. It was crudely wrapped in aluminum foil which was the best he could do in the short time available. "To us," he toasted and handed the box to Eva. She stared at it with tears forming in her eyes. Inside she found an old, scratched, gold wedding band…it was Billy's mothers. He slid it on to her finger. "Marry me."

"It's so beautiful. I am honored to wear it Billy. I love you and always will."

The following morning Billy let Eva sleep in and went to the lobby coffee shop for a much-needed jolt of java. He ordered two to go and returned to his room to call Califano.

"So how do you like the room?" Califano asked.

"Very nice…thank you. So, when do you want to meet?"

"Listen Billy, I'm a little jammed up this morning. Why don't we meet for lunch at Joe Muer's. It's a landmark for seafood here in Detroit. Just take the River

Walk. Shouldn't take more than fifteen minutes. It's a nice day for a walk anyway. Say, 1:30. Good for you?"

Billy thought that would give them time to explore the shops before lunch. "Sounds good. See you then."

Califano was expecting Billy to mention he had a friend with him. No matter. The hit will go down as planned.

Eva woke up as Billy was ending his call. "Hey lover…did you get a coffee for me too?" Billy handed her the still steaming cup and she sipped it carefully. "So what are we doing today?"

"My meeting is set for lunch at a place on the River Walk. We have lots of time to explore this place or you can veg out here in the room." The last remark prompted Eva to grab a pillow and chase her fiancé around the room. The pillow fight ended with a tender embrace and passionate love making.

"I'll be ready in a minute," Eva announced as she jumped in the shower.

Billy had an old canvas messenger bag that he used as a brief case. It was covered with patches from his military deployments but the one that always turned heads was the "Dealer of Death" skull on a playing card. He stuffed his copy of the contract he had previously prepared for his first meeting along with notes he had made on the flight in. “I’m ready when you are.”

CHAPTER 13

The Wild Jokers assassins looked inconspicuous enough in faded jeans and Izod golf shirts under denim blazers. The Uzis were not difficult to conceal, even with the suppressors installed.

They paced off the distance from their selected location to the restaurant and found a park bench facing the river. It was ideal for them although it did not provide the cross fire they had hoped for. It was a beautifully sunny day and they soaked up the rays while watching the pretty office workers head out for lunch. Soon the serenity of an autumn afternoon would explode.

"Come on Eva. You can come back to shop after my meeting." Billy was hungry and it was almost time for him to meet Califano. The Halston shop was filling up with young office workers trying to sneak in some shopping on their lunch breaks. Eva was standing at the three-deep fitting room line and was not about to lose her place.

"Go on. I'll catch up with you as soon as I'm finished here," she yelled.

Billy blew her a kiss and turned to make the short walk to Joe Muers. It took two escalators to get to the street level and the sun almost blinded him as he walked towards the river. The walkway was filled with shoppers from the suburbs and downtown workers with time to kill. It was slow going but Billy didn't mind. He had plenty of time to get to the restaurant.

One of the shooters looked down at his watch and leaned over to his partner who was feeding the pigeons. "Hey numb nuts. Time to get moving." The plan was for one of them to walk ahead until he spotted Billy, then follow him as he approached the other shooter who would make the kill shot. If anything went wrong the man on foot could pursue and finish the job.

After walking about fifty yards, he spotted Billy casually strolling towards him. Billy's shoulder length hair was in a ponytail but there was no doubt it was the man they were sent to kill.

As Billy passed, the shooter waited and then began to follow him, staying no more than twenty feet behind. If it was earlier or later in the afternoon, the number of pedestrians would have been much fewer and Billy would have likely sensed he was being followed.

Billy was approaching the kill zone and was now in view of the shooter on the bench who carefully unbuttoned his jacket and positioned the Uzi on his lap with the barrel facing the river. He had already chambered a round and slowly flicked off the safety. Time to rock and roll.

Billy noticed the man on the bench and thought it unusual for a downtown office worker to be wearing worn and scuffed motorcycle boots. Before he could fully process this anomaly, he heard Eva calling out his name. He turned and saw her running through the crowd with a large Halston bag in her arms. She was smiling and the joy on her face was the last image Billy would have of her as the spit of the Uzi tore through her chest and lungs.

Billy knew instantly the bullets were meant for him and as he stood over Eva he could see two men running up the stairs to the street level. A crowd of people formed around the blood-soaked pavement where Eva lay motionless. She was staring into heaven.

* * *

Stinky Jordan put the phone down then began to slam it on the counter until it shattered into pieces. "You stupid mother fuckers!" he screamed over and over and the clubhouse emptied out quickly. When Stinky loses it, people get hurt. Now he had to deal with major blowback from Califano. It might be him floating in the Detroit River.

The shooters made it back to Windsor and went into hiding after giving Stinky the bad news. They were dead men walking and knew that if they stayed in Windsor, sooner or later Stinky would hunt them down.

Back in Detroit, Billy was lingering in the ER but had already been told that Eva had died at the scene. The doctors had not discovered the fetus until Billy mentioned her being pregnant. It would have been impossible to save either of them…but they confirmed it was a girl.

There was a pay phone in the ER waiting room and Billy called his father, disregarding that it was the middle of the night in Tulsa. "Pop, Califano tried to kill me. It will be on the news soon. Eva was hit and she's gone." He began to cry and never heard his father's words of sorrow. "She was wearing mom's wedding band."

"Bring her home son. Bring her home."

The DPD investigating detective had been patiently waiting for Billy to finish giving his statement. "We need to finish up Billy. I have some pictures for you to look at. You might recognize someone and that would really be helpful."

Billy followed the investigator to his car and made the short drive to the Downtown Service Precinct which was the central hub of the entire force. The Homicide

Department was on the second floor and Billy was amazed at the number of desks and personnel on duty at such a late hour. "Let me get you some coffee. This could take some time."

A few minutes later the detective returned with a large paper cup with steaming coffee. "I hate that shit in the machines. This is from my personal Mister Coffee."

Billy sipped the coffee and the detective motioned for another officer to bring a large photo album over to them. "After you go through these pictures I want to have you sit down with one of our sketch artists who can try and get a rendering we can put out to the media."

"What about the other witnesses?" Billy asked the detective. "Are you bringing them in for questioning? I bet someone got a good look at the two guys as they ran off."

"We have a team of detectives working this case Mr. Whitehorse. Trust me we will pursue every lead and find these guys." Billy was impressed with the dedication he was seeing and now had to deal with getting Eva back to the ones that loved her the most.

After two long days of sitting with the police sketch artist and looking at more pictures it was time for the flight back to Tulsa with Eva. Because of the mandatory autopsy, he decided they would keep the casket closed at the funeral. Once she was at peace, he would seek his vengeance.

* * *

Califano had heard enough and slammed the phone down. It wouldn't take long for Bellante to learn of the failed assassination. What would follow was anyone's guess. There was no plan B and if the shit storm reached all the way up the family ladder, the buck would fall to the lowest rung…Califano. Killing the young Whitehorse was no longer an option. Every swinging dick in law enforcement both in Detroit and Tulsa will be on the lookout.

When the morning paper came out there was no mention of Billy Whitehorse…only the name of the dead girl. If they had made a connection to who the real target was they were keeping it a secret. No motive was listed either. Maybe Califano could keep the connection to killing Whitehorse off Bellante's radar, at least long enough to come up with a new strategy.

What Califano was not considering was Billy seeking revenge. That miscalculation might prove fatal.

* * *

The flight arrived in Tulsa as a new winter storm was hammering the Southwest. Billy's father had arranged to have several tribal members meet the flight and transport Eva's casket back to the reservation. No one said much after the initial hugs and condolences.

Wilson owned one the few pickups with a cover over the truck bed and the cheap casket was loaded into the back. At least it would be protected from the elements as they drove.

As a culture, Cherokee Indians are very spiritual people that view death as a transition rather than an end. Eva's body would not be embalmed. To prepare for burial, the shaman instructed the women to wash and scent the body with lavender oil, believing lavender has strong spiritual properties. Then the washed and scented body was wrapped in a white cotton sheet and placed into a new coffin made from local trees.

Before the funeral began, Billy placed an eagle feather on Eva's body. In most Indian cultures, the eagle is venerated as a sacred bird. Ironically, the shaman was a distant cousin to Eva's mother which enhanced the solemnity of the ceremony.

Once all the mourners were seated, the shaman led them in Cherokee prayers, followed by spiritual lessons on behalf of the living. At this point the funeral would normally end in prayer before the procession to the burial site. Billy chose a different ending, standing over the coffin, holding the wedding band he had place on her finger only days before. He had put it on a silver necklace.

"This is the ring I gave Eva when I asked her to be my wife. She was wearing it proudly when she was killed. Most of you did not know that she was carrying my child…a girl." A soft murmur went through the crowd. They were mourning two deaths that day. Billy put the necklace over his head and the ring hung directly over his heart. "Let us carry my wife to her resting place." The selected members of the tribe picked up the coffin, placing it on their shoulders for the long walk to the burial ground.

Traditionally the Cherokee have a seven-day mourning period under the auspices of the shaman. This period is considered a spiritual cleansing time for the survivors. During this time, family members are not allowed to be angry or jovial and must restrict their intake of food and water.

Billy spent that time in solitude, taking Eva's truck into the desert, watching the sun move across the sky day after day. When he returned, he was seriously dehydrated and delusional but insisted on joining the shaman and mourners in the traditional river bathing. Seven times they immersed themselves, altering direction of facing east then west. After the ceremony, Billy was given fresh clothes, tobacco and sacred beads. Only then was he welcomed back into the tribe.

CHAPTER 14

The funeral was fit for a president or head of state. Damon spared no expense giving his father the sendoff he had earned his entire life. What Wilfred Drummond had lacked as a parent he more than made up for as a stalwart member of the community. Charities all across Dallas and the entire state benefitted from his generosity. Sadly, that was coming to an end with Damon controlling the purse strings.

Wilfred Drummond's death occurred after Damon had filed for bankruptcy on the Palace. Any initial damage to the family name was lost in the financial sector that was now preoccupied with how Damon would change the company he inherited. His attorneys were masters at keeping the blowback from the bankruptcy from impacting the company Damon was now running.

First order of business was to payoff Aubrey Bennison before he stole the Miss USA Pageant. As soon as that check was written, Damon filed the necessary papers to change the casino name to Drummond Palace.

All the contractors that were stiffed from the bankruptcy were replaced and the renovations went forward at record speed to accommodate the new "Grand Opening" which would coincide with the beauty pageant.

The second order of business was to move the corporate headquarters to Nevada once the pageant was over. He had already put the offices in Dallas on the market and expected to make a tidy profit on the ensuing sale. Any staff that refused to relocate were fired…regardless of seniority or position. Damon chose to reward Jill Beauville and made her Executive VP of the entire Drummond empire. Her brother was passed over and would remain in his current position. Jill had no problem with that decision.

The problem of the new Indian casino was still on Damon's radar although they had yet to break ground. Word on the street was that the mob was trying to get a piece of the new operation but was having problems closing the sale. Damon wasn't worried. He was confident that the new Drummond Palace would eclipse any current or future competition in the Laughlin area.

* * *

Billy had reached out to the Detroit Police several times since the funeral but they still had no hard suspects or even a motive. Billy knew the motive but kept that to himself…better to avoid any connection to him when Califano was paid a visit.

Wilson chose to give Billy plenty of space as he mourned the loss of Eva. The Fort Mohave Tribe was very sensitive to what Wilson and his family were going through and put everything on hold. Every evening Billy would walk to Eva's burial site and lay beside her, staring at the stars and wondering what their life together would have been like. Slowly, sorrow had turned to blind hatred and Wilson could see in his son's eyes that another trip to Detroit was on the horizon.

Califano eventually got the call he was dreading…" Mr. Bellante needs to see you." The sit down was to take place at Bellante's home in Gross Pointe. The stately mansion was on Lake Shore Drive, next door to the old Edsel Ford home that was now a museum. Having a full blown Mafia Don in the neighborhood raised no eyebrows. Gross Pointe had long been a magnet to the newly rich gentry class and no one demanded a resume for entry.

As Vincent passed through the gates and drove down the long driveway, he knew this might be his last day on the planet. Sal had insisted that he be picked up by one of his personal limos…another bad sign. As they neared the circular driveway in front of the main entrance, Vincent noticed two other parked limos. Very unusual.

Califano was greeted by one of the mansion staff and led to the large patio where two men were sitting and smoking cigars and two others stood quietly behind their chairs. It was much too cold for an outdoor meeting but Vincent would be the last to complain.

"Vinnie, come have a seat. I got the fire pit started so it will be nice and comfy." Sal was not sending any signals that Califano could pick up on but that meant nothing. The kiss on the cheek could easily be the prelude to a knife in the back.

One of the attendees was a surprise. It was Jackie Zerilli, Joseph's youngest son and designated heir to the throne. Jackie's older brother Carmen had chosen the priesthood instead of following his father's tarnished life style which Jackie embraced.

"You know Jackie, right?" Bellante asked as Califano took his seat.

"Sure, sure. Hi Jackie. Good to see you again," came Vinnie's reply.

Bellante offered Vinnie a cigar, Havana for sure, and sat back without saying a word.

Jackie swirled the brandy in his glass several times before taking a sip while the others watched. "So Vincent Califano…Sal tells me you fucked up this casino thing big time." Vinnie started to speak and Jackie held a finger to his lips, a clear signal to shut up.

"You know Vinnie, we never asked you to provide muscle…just brains and the skill to keep things clean and profitable. And you've done this very well. To clean up the stalemate with the Indians you went to Sal and he gave you the greenlight for the hit. Am I right so far?"

"Yes Jackie. That's pretty much the story," Vinnie answered, not sure where Jackie was going with this. He looked over at Sal who was looking down at his hands, cleaning his nails, totally relaxed.

Each of the two who were standing moved discreetly behind Sal and Vinnie's chairs…never taking their eyes off Jackie.

Jackie continued. "Would you agree Vinnie that you really aren't the hard ass type. You're more of a numbers guy. That's what you and your company does for us. Right?"

"Yeah Jackie we do our best. The profits have been very good. But you know that." Vinnie could see the breath of the man standing behind him in the cold night air.

He guessed the last sound he would hear would be the spit of the bullet as it entered his brain.

Suddenly the man behind Sal slipped a wire garrote around his neck and pulled. As Sal slid from his chair Jackie spoke again. “Sal should have known better. You stupid fuck! You don’t send a bean counter to war. Congratulations Vinnie. You just got a promotion. Tony, get this piece of shit out of my sight.” The two soldiers lifted Sal’s body and carried it to a waiting skiff by the dock where they started the small outboard and disappeared into the night.

* * *

Aubrey Bennison didn’t lose…period. When he got Drummond’s check, he was livid that the little prick was able to use his dad’s death to bail him out. He decided then and there that his life’s mission was to bury Damon Drummond and piss on his financial grave.

He had requested a detailed report on the Fort Mohave Tribe and, specifically, the facts on its cash flow and other hard assets. All Jews had a soft spot for the plight of the American Indian. Both shared a legacy of oppression and genocide. Both were proud people determined to never let another race subrogate their right to survive.

Aubrey's lead attorney had prepared a summary that was easy to understand. The tribe had significant land holdings and invested wisely in the infant tech revolution that was generating sizeable liquidity. They shared a dream with the Cherokee's of Oklahoma to take advantage of the recent new legislation opening the gaming industry to their people. Pooling their money gave them enough to start construction but not enough to finish.

The report also confirmed that serious negotiations had begun with a Detroit front for the Zerilli mob family. Those discussions appeared to be stalled due to the death of a member of the tribe's family. "OK they need money," Aubrey said to himself. "That I got."

Bennison instructed his secretary to set up a meeting as soon as possible with Shan Williams.

CHAPTER 15

Intimate conversation between Billy and his father rarely occurred. Billy went off to war against his father's wishes and compounded the resentment by redeploying until the fall of Saigon. The fact that he came home a highly decorated hero carried no weight between them. He had abandoned his people to fight another man's war.

One would think the tragic death of Eva would have brought them together to seek revenge but that was not in Wilson's DNA. He had the wisdom of an elder but not the spirit of a warrior. Billy would fulfill that role.

"I'll be gone for a while, father. It is better that you don't know where I am going. Your responsibility is to maintain the status quo until I get back." Billy was not asking for approval…he was giving a command.

"They say revenge is a dish best served cold, Billy. Be careful and go slow. I need you back here as soon as possible."

Billy kissed his father's forehead and waited for the taxi to take him to the airport. He did not want to transport any weapons as luggage. The red tape would create a red flag that could be followed in an investigation. Instead he decided to ship his AR-15 and Colt 1911 to the Ramada where he had stayed on his first trip to Detroit. They would be waiting for him under the name of Terry Bishop who was a fallen comrade from the battle of Hue. He would throw in a few clips of ammo as well.

The mood in Detroit was festive and the hotels were fully displaying their best Christmas decorations. The larger the hotel, the more lavish the decorations. It was unseasonably warm for December and any snow that had fallen was gone.

When the shuttle pulled up to the Ramada, Billy was flooded with memories of his last visit and specifically Karen. He also was vigilant to any sign of her pimp, assuming that if she was there, Sugar was sure to follow. He went to the front desk and saw no one that was around when he last visited. "You have a reservation for Terry Bishop."

The clerk punched in some data and found the confirmation. "Yes sir Mr. Bishop. I have you staying five nights. Is that correct?"

"Yes…five nights. Also, you should be holding a couple of packages for me."

The clerk handed Billy a sign-in sheet. "What card would you like to use Mr. Bishop?"

"I'll be paying in cash. How about I give you three nights in advance and we play the rest by ear." The clerk was confused and not sure how to proceed. He never received payment in cash before.

"Give me a second to check with my supervisor." He walked to the back room and returned with an elderly black woman wearing a *Manager* badge on her vest.

"I'm sorry for the delay Mr. Bishop. Ronnie has never had a guest pay in cash before." She picked up the loose bills Billy had placed on the counter and handed him his room key. "I'll have someone bring your packages to your room in a few minutes. Enjoy your stay and be sure and let us know if you need anything."

Billy smiled and walked to the bank of elevators, careful to avoid looking in to the bar area. His room was on the fourth floor and directly across from the vending and ice machines. The television had been upgraded since his last visit and now included a box for ordering movies.

He laid his bag on the bed and carefully unpacked, hanging each shirt and pair of pants on a hanger and placing his toiletry items on the bathroom sink. He was almost anal in how he arranged his personal grooming items…razor, shaving cream, comb, aftershave, toothbrush, toothpaste and his own shampoo and conditioner.

In another leather pouch he withdrew items to attend to battle wounds…peroxide, bandages, scissors, suture needles and thread. He brought a prescription for oxycodone but, having a high tolerance for pain, he rarely saw the need for medication.

As he was completing his inventory there was a knock on the door. His packages had arrived. He gave the young man a sizeable tip which was earned because the disassembled weapons and the ammo was heavy to carry.

His small pocket knife was barely capable of cutting through the layers of tape but it was virtually impossible for anyone to have guessed what the boxes contained and the packaging served that purpose well.

Billy was his normal fastidious self in inspecting each piece of the weapons as he reassembled them. Satisfied that the rifle and handgun were in perfect working order he slid the weapons under his mattress and called down for room service. "Sorry sir. Room service ended at 7:30. The restaurant will be open until 10:00 if you want to come down for dinner. We begin serving breakfast at 7:00 am."

Billy was hoping to avoid even a chance encounter with Karen but now that option was out the window if he wanted to eat. It was time to see if his wise council was followed or ignored by the young girl he had befriended. He lifted the mattress and pulled out the Colt then slipped a loaded clip in and racked a round. He slid the hand gun into his waist and under his shirt and walked to the elevator.

Stepping off into the lobby area Billy peeked into the bar before walking to the restaurant. He saw several men, probably salesmen, sitting at bar watching the hockey game and yelling as the teams scrambled across the ice. He never understood that game and preferred football which he excelled at in high school before enlisting. No sign of Karen. That was a good thing.

Someone had left the day's edition of the Detroit Free Press on an empty booth and Billy grabbed it to read as he ate. He ordered a well-done T-bone with loaded baked potato and green beans and washed it down with a local beer…Stroh's which was horrible but did the job. After his second beer, he charged the meal to his room and decided to venture to the bar, fingers crossed that Karen would not be there.

By now the bar was full, mostly salesmen types enjoying the game and shop talk. Billy took a seat at a small table along the wall with a panoramic view of the entire bar. That evening a waitress was taking drink orders which kept the bar tender running all night. Billy recognized him but there was nothing visible to indicate he recognized Billy.

"What will you have?" the waitress asked impatiently and Billy ordered another Stroh's. He was acquiring a taste for it. As she took his order and walked back to the bar Billy scanned the room slowly and, again, saw no sign of Karen or her pimp. Thank God. Now he might be able to get a full night's sleep.

When the girl returned with his beer, Billy decided to give it one last try. "Excuse me miss but I was wondering about a friend who used to hang out here awhile back."

"What was his name?" she asked in reply.

"Actually it was a girl…a very young girl…probably underage. The name she gave me was Karen. Not sure if that is her real name."

"Are you a cop?" she answered, eager to end the conversation.

"No…just a friend who is worried about her. That's all."

The waitress walked away to tend to other customers but returned in about five minutes.

"If you are such a good friend you would be visiting her hospital room instead of this place."

Billy was totally caught off guard even though, in his gut, he knew that would be the outcome if she returned to her old life. "What happened to her?" He knew what the answer would be.

"We found her in the parking lot one morning. She had her jaw broken and had a fractured skull. She was in bad shape. Someone beat the shit out of her. She is in the physical therapy wing of Oakwood Hospital. Been there for almost a month."

"Can she have visitors? I'd like to check in on her while I'm in town."

"Yeah she can have visitors. Would probably like to see another face besides mine but if you are some sick fuck wanting to see when his favorite hooker will be back on the job you need to get lost."

"You have it all wrong. I know what she did for a living but I never was a customer. Like I said…just a friend she met along the way. I also have a pretty good idea who beat her but it's her call on bringing in the police. I would have expected that to have already happened."

The waitress had to take another drink order and stepped away. Billy sipped his beer while he waited for her to return.

"Look I have to break this off. We are pretty packed tonight because of the game. I assume you are staying here so if you want to go with me to see Karen tomorrow morning be in the lobby…say around 10 am. By the way, my name is Gloria. See you tomorrow."

Billy called it a night and returned to his room. He was looking forward to seeing Karen again…then he would pay a call on Sugar. It was beginning to look like his stay in Detroit would be longer than planned.

CHAPTER 16

Billy was up early and ordered room service for breakfast. He had a couple of hours to kill until Gloria picked him up. In the meantime, he called Califano's office to see if he was in town. "Mr. Califano's office…can I help you?" The voice sounded like the same one that met him and escorted him to the inner sanctum of Califano and Company.

"Is he taking appointments today?" Billy asked as though he was a regular associate.

"Sorry…his schedule is booked up for the next two days. May I take your name and let him know you called?"

"No thanks. I'll try again in a few days." OK, he would get a shot at Califano. He would need to get some wheels as he would need to do some recon on Califano's movements to isolate the best place for their "reunion".

It was almost ten so Billy grabbed his jacket, the 1911 snugly in his waist band, and went to the lobby where Gloria was already waiting in a red Mustang convertible. "Good…you're on time. Hop in. The hospital is not that far and traffic should be light at this hour."

"Nice ride," Billy commented as he squeezed in to the passenger's seat.

"Thanks. I had to slam a lot of beer across the bar to earn this baby. Every working girl deserves a red convertible don't you think?"

"Yes indeed. I have an old Trans Am but nowhere near as nice as this."

Gloria turned up the radio to WKNR, an FM station playing nothing but the best rock and, in this case, the Eagles "Take it Easy" blared from the stereo speakers…clearly not factory issued. Gloria sang along loudly, knowing every line of the lyrics. Twenty minutes and five songs later they pulled into the parking lot of the hospital.

Billy followed Gloria through the lobby and down a long corridor to another wing where the PT and Rehab area was located. Room after room had numerous patients on various machines designed to hasten their recovery. In every case, each patient was watched closely by a staff member who guided and prodded them to the next level.

"Been a long time since I was in a place like this. I like being a visitor a lot more than being a patient." Billy's flashback did not go unnoticed by Gloria.

"I noticed the scars on your cheek and arm. Guess you saw some bad shit in Vietnam. Glad you made it home in one piece."

"Why did you assume I got these scars in Nam?"

"My brother served and got two purple hearts. You both have that 1000-mile stare. It scares me, I'll be honest. It never left him…even when he was spit on and yelled at when he flew home. He swore he would never put on his uniform again."

"Unless you were there you can never understand. I get that, but we were warriors sent to do a job and we did it. For that we at least deserved a kind smile and thank you. That's all." Billy was done strolling down memory lane. He saw Karen using a treadmill and his heart broke. She was working up quite a sweat and took a second for her eyes to focus on Billy through the glass. Then she began to cry.

Billy entered the training room, leaving Gloria behind and walked up to Karen who hung her head, still in tears. She was wearing a wire that connected her upper and lower teeth together. Being on a liquid diet had taken its toll on her weight and general fitness. "My God…Karen! Did Sugar do this to you?"

She couldn't talk but nodded her head. Gloria heard the question and tried to protect the girl. "Leave the kid alone. She's lucky to be alive. Knowing who did this won't make her heal any faster." She hugged Karen and asked the therapist when she would be able to eat regular food again.

"You'll have to ask her doctor but I think she is almost there," was the reply.

Billy left the room and walked to the nurse station. "Is the doctor around?" he asked one of the nurses who was busy entering data into a computer.

"There are several doctors. Which one are you looking for?"

"The one who is treating Karen…sorry, I don't know her last name." Billy looked suspicious to the young nurse who was about to call security when Gloria walked up.

"He's with me. Is Doctor Patel around? We would like an update on Karen Whitmer."

The nurse asked what appeared to be the head nurse where the doctor was and was told he was doing rounds in the main part of the hospital. He would not be visiting the PT wing today. "Sorry but I can look at her chart and see what it shows." The young nurse was trying to be helpful.

"OK. The doctor was here yesterday and he will be removing the jaw wiring tomorrow. Her range of motion and mobility is back to normal and the skull fracture has healed enough to confirm no further signs of concussion.

We need to fatten her up a little before he releases her. This is all good news. She's been through a lot for such a young girl."

This report was the first piece of good news Billy had heard in quite some time. After speaking to the nurses, Billy walked with Karen to her room…holding her as gently as a new born baby. Karen climbed into bed and Billy and Gloria sat down to keep her company for a while although the communications were only one sided.

"Karen, I wish you would have taken my advice and left this place for good. Sugar and his crew are bad people. They enjoy hurting those that can't defend themselves. I've faced bullies like that my entire life and they need to feel pain…bad pain before they get the message."

Karen shook her head "no" but Billy wasn't finished. "Don't worry Karen. They will never hurt you again…I promise. They just need to be taught a lesson. Get well. I'll be back to see you before you're released." Gloria whispered something in Karen's ear and followed Billy out to the parking lot.

Once in the car, Gloria told Billy what was on her mind. "Look Terry or whatever your name is. The people you think did this to Karen are killers. I've watched Sugar operate in my bar for over a year. He picks the young ones and they depend on him for everything. To Karen he was the only reliable person in her life and she took all his abuse because she had no other options. If you intend to become an option in her life it will require a hell of a lot more than just kicking some pimp's ass. So don't open that door unless you are willing to accept all the baggage that comes with it."

Billy was impressed. Gloria was wise beyond her young age and what she said was true. The rage he was feeling was partially attributable to the loss of Eva and it was carrying over to Karen. He was committed to getting payback for both women…starting with Karen.

Gloria was going to drop Billy off back at the Ramada but he needed to rent a car and asked her to take him back to the airport baggage claim. "Thanks Gloria. I'll see you soon but if Sugar shows up at the Ramada please leave me a message for my room."

"Will do Mister Badass. Be careful." Gloria waved goodbye and Billy headed to the Avis counter.

* * *

From the outside, the abandoned house with the boarded windows and weed infested front yard looked like all the others in the Highland Park area. Billy had been driving his rental Olds Sierra up and down the deserted streets looking for Sugar's gold El Dorado…and there it sat. In years past, a street light would be beaming down on the exact spot where the car sat. Tonight it was only reflecting the full moon in the shiny gold paint.

Billy stopped about half a block from the house and went to his trunk. The AR-15 was wrapped in newspaper but the clip was already inserted. Billy chambered a round and closed the trunk, looking to see if any eyes were watching. So far so good.

The neighborhood was so infested with crack houses that the police usually just drove past, preferring to keep the trash in one spot. Only when it spilled out into white or mixed communities did they deploy and start busting skulls. That was why no lookouts were posted by the house making it easy for Billy to breach a back window.

It was a cloudless night and the moon illuminated the room enough for Billy to get his bearings. There was a short hallway leading to the kitchen which was empty and littered with trash and animal feces. Billy could hear voices coming from the second level and as he approached the stairs he could hear the O'Jays blasting through a large boom box. *'People all over the world, join in, on a love train…love train'*. Billy knew every lyric as it was played over and over by his black brothers recuperating from wounds in the 95th Evacuation Hospital at the base of Monkey Mountain south of Da Nang.

The stairs were old and creaked with every step but the music hid the sound Billy was making and he reached the upper landing unnoticed. Ahead was another hall with several bedrooms and a bathroom at the far end. Tactically, Billy was in the best firing position right where he was standing. He just needed to lure the target to the kill zone.

He backed up to the last step and knelt with the rifle resting on the landing floor. "Hey cocksucker!" he screamed loud enough to be heard over the music. "Sugar…you chicken shit mother fucker!" he called out even louder and suddenly the music stopped. He could hear people shuffling around and furniture moving. Slowly a head appeared with the biggest afro Billy had ever seen. It wasn't Sugar but he recognized the man as one that came to greet him with Sugar on his last trip.

The man's chrome plated revolver gleamed in the moonlight and Billy delivered five rounds into the man who was thrown back into the bedroom. Then all hell broke loose.

CHAPTER 17

The first wave came at Billy, guns firing wildly and missing him completely as he was shooting from ground level in the stair well. They took the .223 rounds in the chest and head and fell in a bloody heap no more than 10 feet from Billy. There was a lull before the next shots started flying, this time from the entrance to one of the bedrooms. This gave Billy just enough time to reload the AR before returning fire.

The shooters had learned the lesson of their fallen comrades and did their best to stay behind cover. Billy guessed the old dry wall couldn't stop his shots so he peppered the wall with gunfire and the ensuing silence gave him a good indication his shots had found their targets. He had emptied the second rifle clip and pulled out the .45 which gave him seven rounds in each of his two clips.

In the silence, Billy could hear the panting of someone trying to breathe through pain...someone in the process of dying. Moving slowly down the dark hallway, Billy stepped over the bodies and inched towards the sound he was hearing. Peeking into the room he saw two more bodies and a third in a fetal position against the wall leading to the bathroom. This one was still alive and gasping for breath…probably from a shot to the chest. He had a stainless Colt Python cradled in his lap but he didn't have enough strength to pick it up.

Billy kept his pistol trained on the survivor and walked close enough to see the man's face. It was Sugar and he was spitting blood and began to scream when he recognized Billy. "What the fuck are you doing man? Do you love the skinny bitch? Is that it?" Billy reached down and took the .357 from Sugar. It still had three rounds in it.

"Get me to a hospital and I'll get you all the pussy you want and plenty of cash to go with it." Sugar could see in Billy's eyes that there was no bargain to be made and he began to crawl into the bathroom in desperation. Billy watched him and saw the pool of blood growing larger in his wake.

"From the looks of your wounds I'd guess you are in a hell of a lot of pain little brother. I've seen lots of guys with belly shots and it is not an easy way to die. My guess is you have about another thirty minutes before you bleed out. I would love to stay and watch you die but my guess is all the noise may have woken up a neighbor with a phone and five-o is on the way."

Billy picked up the AR and the empty magazine and stood over Sugar close enough to whisper in his ear. "Man

I love the O'Jays. Every time I hear one of their songs I'm gonna think of you." He held his hand above the muzzle of the .45 to block the blood blowback and squeezed the trigger. *"Do things, do things, do things bad things with it…money money money money"* Billy sung as he quickly jumped down the stairs and ran to his car. As he pulled away he could see the flashing lights in the distance.

For the first time in weeks, Billy was feeling good about himself…good about what he had done for somebody else. The remorse he had felt for taking a life in war wasn't there this time. Those punks were not fighting for their country like the VC. They were bottom dwellers, the worst of what man can produce and he was the exterminator.

With his car radio tuned to WCHB, a stream of R&B and Disco tunes made the drive back to the Ramada go quickly. He left the AR in the trunk and walked through an empty lobby to the elevators. The bar was empty as was the restaurant. Too late for a midnight snack so off to bed he went where he would sleep soundly for a change.

The following morning Billy slept longer than usual. He knew he had time to kill before Gloria's shift started so he decided to do some recon on Califano, starting with locating his private residence. There was no listing with the phone company which was not surprising. The best option would be to follow him from his office but that would require hours of idle stakeout time.

As he considered his options his phone rang. It was Gloria calling from the hospital. "Terry, its Gloria. Did you see the news last night? There was quite a shootout at some crack house in Highland Park. One of the victims was identified as Mario Clairborne, aka Sugar."

"So you're calling me with good news. How nice. How's Karen? Did she get the wires removed from her jaw?"

"Don't fuck with me Terry. It's beyond coincidental that Sugar was killed right after you saw Karen. I am the last person to judge you for what you did if you did it. I haven't told Karen yet. Thought maybe I would leave that to you."

"Thanks. I have a pretty full plate today so I'll come by the hospital tomorrow. Karen is lucky to have you as a friend."

After a late breakfast Billy stopped at a nearby sporting goods store and bought 100 rounds of .223 ammo, one box of .45 hollow points and a pair of high power Bushnell binoculars. He loaded the two empty clips and threw them in the trunk before driving down to the Renaissance Center and parking in a lot with an unobstructed view of the office towers and hotel exits. The binoculars gave him a good look at everyone coming out of the buildings. They would have to pass his line of sight to reach the various parking areas as well as the train stop on the river.

He guessed that a man of Califano's wealth and stature would use a limo for travel to and from his home. He would focus his attention on those waiting curbside. If that failed, he would have to spend a long week of sitting and watching.

After waiting for more than three hours, Billy got lucky. A black stretch limo arrived curbside at about 7:00 pm and the driver opened the rear door and stood waiting. Billy was sure that under his black cashmere top coat was at least one hand gun at the ready. Moments later Califano exited the tower and climbed in to the limo.

Billy started his car and sped to catch up to the limo as it exited on to the Lodge Freeway heading East and then North on to I-75. Billy followed at a safe distance, helped by the heavy commuter traffic leaving the downtown area. The farther north they traveled the lighter the traffic became and made it more difficult to follow without being noticed.

As they entered Bloomfield Hills, Billy saw the best examples of lavish new money opulence. Winding asphalt roads were dotted by one-acre home sites nestled in tree covered cul-de-sacs. Finally, the limo turned on to Lahser Road and pulled up to a tall wrought iron gate. Across the road stood the prestigious Cranbrook Academy of Art, a National Historic Landmark founded in the early 20th century by newspaper mogul George Gough Booth.

Billy parked and watched the limo driver enter a code that opened the gate, allowing the car to proceed down a long driveway. With the binoculars, Billy could see the limo park in front of a pillared mansion worthy of a civil war novel. The driver got out and then opened the rear door for the passenger who paid his salary.

Billy pulled away and turned on to Woodward Avenue looking for a place to grab a bite and consider his options. To his right was a crowded drive-in burger place called Ted's and he pulled in to a space that had just emptied. Pretty basic menu, he thought, and ordered a cheeseburger and chocolate milk shake.

As he ate, he was amazed at the number of hot cars that slowly cruised through with all eyes focused on the most tricked out rides. Billy's first car was a very old '57 Chevy Bel Air and he saw a pristine version slowly drive past. Someday, he thought, he would own another one of these classics.

Turning his attention back to Califano, he recognized that once he passed through his gate he would be difficult if not impossible to get to. Chances were very good that the property had a very elaborate security system that may even include dogs…and Billy hated guard dogs. Even if he could get his hands on a small amount of C-4, the explosion would quickly draw a crowd of law enforcement and firemen. His best option was a car bomb.

Billy remembered the Brinks Hotel bombing in Saigon. The VC had loaded about 200 pounds of explosives in the trunk of a car and parked it with a timer set to detonate at the peak of happy hour. It worked to perfection but the body count was much lower than the enemy had hoped for. Billy had duplicated that event several times against the NVA and could do it again. All he needed was some gasoline and a quick trip to the hardware store.

* * *

Billy opened his trunk and took out the two plastic bags he had obtained during his trip to Ace Hardware. He also carried the plastic gas can that he had filled before coming back to the Ramada. No one paid attention to him as he walked through the lobby and entered the elevator. Once settled in his room, he cleared off the small table and moved it next to the bed where he had laid out everything he purchased earlier.

First step was to place some of the caulking compound into the large glass jar he had purchased. Next he filled it halfway with gasoline and let it set until the caulking had dissolved. Once everything was completed dissolved he added about 3 ounces of motor oil.

After most of the gasoline mixture evaporated, he put on rubber gloves and began to knead the compound into a pliable mixture and rolled it into long thin strips which he let sit for two hours. Next he kneaded it again…let it set five minutes and repeated the process until the gasoline could no longer be smelled. The final product was a white to light gray plastic with the consistency of stiff putty. His homemade C-4 was born.

He checked his Casio F-91W digital watch and saw that Gloria should be manning the bar by now. He would need to replace the Casio, as it would be converted into a timer to detonate the C-4.

He took a quick shower to get the smell of bomb preparation off his skin and hair and then rode the elevator down to the lobby. He left his Colt under the mattress.

CHAPTER 18

Shan stood and watched his visitor use his cane to maneuver down the stairs to his Bentley. His driver assisted him into the car and they drove slowly away back to Las Vegas, kicking up a huge dust cloud until they reached the highway.

Shan needed to get Wilson Whitehorse on the phone right away with the good news. "Wilson, its Shan. Our tribe continues to mourn for your loss. I hope Billy is adapting. I can't imagine what he is feeling right now."

"Good to hear from you Shan and thanks for your patience during this difficult period. We have all returned to our normal routine except for Billy. Once the mourning period ended he took off without telling anyone but I am sure he is seeking revenge for Eva. Pray that he returns safely my friend."

"I understand." Shan replied. "Billy is a warrior and warriors are always searching for the next battle. He will not find peace until this is over…peace in life or peace in death. There is no other way for him."

Wilson considered his young friend's words but could not find any of his own to respond. "So what is going on Shan?"

"I just had a meeting with Aubrey Bennison. He heard we are looking for investors and wants to jump in. Looks like his deal with Drummond blew up and he wants some payback."

"That's great news Shan. How big a piece does he want?"

"We never got that far Wilson. He was on a fishing expedition to see if we would be open to an offer. I told him I needed to talk to you first. I think we can shuffle the cards any way we want. Drummond is throwing around his inheritance like a drunken sailor on shore leave, and Bennison wants to humiliate him…sooner rather than later. He wants us to have an Oscar night type of ground-breaking ceremony the same night as the Miss USA Pageant."

"I don't see the connection Shan." Wilson hadn't heard that the pageant was being held at the Palace Casino.

"That will be Damon's big night…the re-opening of his flagship resort under his own name. He has invited every high-roller on his rolodex and Dick Clark is the M/C. If we steal the spot light he will be disgraced and labeled a clown."

"I like this option Shan but I would really like to wait until Billy gets back. His life was destroyed trying to get this casino built. I owe him this much."

Shan was sympathetic to Wilson's request. "I'll stall him as long as I can but we may have to take a second meeting and you need to be there, with or without Billy."

* * *

Billy stood in the entrance to the Ramada bar and studied the patrons for any stragglers from Sugar's gang of thugs. The crowd was lily white except for one of the bar maids. Gloria was busy and didn't notice Billy when he first sat down. The black waitress placed a small napkin in front of Billy. "What can I get you?" she asked.

"How about a double black-jack and coke. And ask Gloria to come over when she has a chance." Jack Daniels and Coke was the go-to drink of Billy's platoon and he never lost his taste for the sweet concoction.

Billy took a sip of his drink as Gloria slid next to him in his booth. Billy had never really paid much attention to Gloria's appearance. She was in her early 30's, pretty fit with red hair which appeared to be natural. Not a bad looking girl.

"Hey there Rambo. Did you have a nice day? I thought you were coming by the hospital?"

"I had some important business to take care of and lost track of time. How is Karen today?"

"She looks great. Wires are out and she can't stop eating. She has to be under 100 pounds so fattening her up is the first priority. They want to discharge her tomorrow but she is scared to death that Sugar will find her again. I haven't told her anything yet."

"Look, before we go any further I want to tell you my real name. It's Billy Whitehorse but you can't tell anyone. It could get me killed, OK?"

Gloria was confused but didn't have time to get into it. "Sure, OK but you have to tell Karen about what you did. She needs to know she is safe."

"I understand. Where is she going to stay when she gets discharged? I gave her a shitload of cash when I left last time. Unless she gave it all to Sugar, she should have enough to get a place in a decent area of the city."

"I don't know where to take her. Sugar had her and his others girls stashed at some flea bag hotel on John R. All her things are still there. If she has that money you gave her it's probably gone. I don't have anything to give her. I'm trying to raise a kid on a barmaid's tips."

Billy knew there was only one good option. "OK, she can stay with me for a few days. I'll find her a place."

Billy pulled out his wallet and handed Gloria his credit card. "Can you use this to buy her some clothes and whatever else she might need.? Just drop it by for me when you come to work tomorrow night."

Gloria took his credit card a gave him a gentle kiss. "You're a good man Billy Whitehorse."

Billy finished his drink and returned to his room to construct the detonator using his Casio watch. The watch timer went up to 24 hours so he had a lot of latitude in deciding when to kill Vincent Califano. It took him another hour to install the watch face and the other components to the small circuit board and it was done. He would plant the bomb on the limo when it went to pick up Califano. The only problem was creating a diversion to get the driver away from the vehicle long enough for Billy to attach the I.E.D.

Before retiring for the night, Billy packed the bomb and a roll of duct tape in his back pack and put all the materials he had used into a plastic ACE Hardware bag which he would dispose of in the morning. He needed the room to be clear before he brought Karen back to stay.

* * *

Billy arrived at the hospital right after Karen had finished her breakfast. Gloria was also there, helping

Karen apply some makeup to her still bruised cheek when Billy walked in to her room. The girl sitting in front of him looked nothing like the one he found in the Ramada bar. Karen looked like a high school girl in her white sweat shirt and denim jeans which were too short…probably Gloria's. Her ash blonde hair was in a ponytail, adding to the youthful appearance.

"Karen, you look beautiful!" Billy announced when she saw him. He had bought a cheap bouquet of yellow daffodils in the hospital gift shop and handed them to her, getting a kiss and hug in return.

"Oh Billy. Thank you for coming. I should have taken your advice and got on that airplane to Chicago but I was so alone and afraid."

"I understand, but it almost got you killed." Billy continued to hold her to his chest.

"I know and he can still finish what he started, Billy. I'm scared to death." Karen was now shaking in fear of what the future may have in store for her.

"Gloria, could you give us a moment?" Billy thought it best to make it seem as though he was sharing something with Karen that no one else knew. Gloria read between the lines and left to get a cup of coffee.

Karen sat on the edge of her bed facing Billy, totally confused as to what he might have to say that Gloria couldn't hear. "What is it?"

"If you saw the news the other night there was a report on an incident in Highland Park. There was a shootout at a notorious crack house and several dealers were killed. One of them was your friend Sugar."

Karen gasped in amazement at what she just heard. "Are you serious? Are you sure it was Sugar?"

"I'm sure Karen…because I was there."

"What? You were there? Why Billy? I don't understand."

"He had to pay for what he did to you Karen…for what he did to God knows how many other young girls he plucked off the bus, or train. I didn't want you to have to live with his shadow hanging over you. You may not agree with what I did now, but later you will see it was the right thing to do."

Karen was speechless and sat in silence contemplating what Billy had said. "I guess I should thank you but it really was none of your business. No one asked you to get involved. Well now you're stuck with me. I have no place to go…no money…nothing. Does Gloria know?"

"She knows what she saw on television but not that I was involved. Let's keep it that way." Gloria returned right on cue and knew that Billy had explained about Sugar.

"They have you all processed and ready to go Karen. Let's go shopping. We'll meet Billy later at his hotel." Karen followed Gloria and Billy to the parking lot and drove off. Billy opened his trunk, took out his Colt and slipped it under his shirt. He needed one last recon trip before going to battle.

* * *

Billy was in the bar when Gloria and Karen returned pulling two rolling suitcases that appeared to be bulging with new clothes. None of the bar patrons recognized Karen who still looked like a teenager that just got out of class for the day. "Here's your credit card Billy. Karen has all the receipts in her new purse. We tried to go cheap but you know us girls."

"Thanks. I hope they don't decline my card when I try to get gas." Billy was happy that Karen was happy.

Gloria went to get her apron and punch in and Karen followed Billy to the elevator with both suitcases in tow. The room had been cleaned and the bags with all the leftover bomb making materials was gone. Well the cleaning people obviously thought it was trash because Billy had placed them on top of the small trash can under the desk.

"Well this will be your home for the next few days so unpack whatever you need. There's a cot in the closet that I'll use so the bed is all yours." Karen unzipped one of the suitcases and took out some flannel pajamas and fresh bra and panties for the next day.

"I thought we would order room service for dinner. We have a lot of catching up to do if you're up to it." He handed her the room service menu and went to the bathroom to wash up.

When he returned, Karen was watching television. "I ordered for both of us. I hope you like steak."

Their meals arrived thirty minutes later and they dove into the steaks, finishing off the meal with a cold Miller's…her favorite. "Look Billy, I probably was a little unappreciative earlier but Gloria filled in the blanks and I know now that without your help I would be dead. I want to show my appreciation the only way I know how." She came to him and sat on his lap, her small breast almost touching his mouth through the t-shirt she had changed into. Her nipples were hard with a growing passion and when she lowered her mouth to his, he returned her kiss with all of the pent-up emotion he had been carrying since Eva's death.

The lovemaking was long and rough. Karen used all her skills to take Billy to places of ecstasy he only dreamed about. When it was over they both lay, sweating and out of breath. "Are you happy Billy?" she asked, stroking him to another erection and he answered with another round of lovemaking. They repeated this routine until early morning.

CHAPTER 19

The new lovers slept in late, exhausted from the lovemaking that kept them up half the night. Karen was up first and made coffee in the small carafe that was supplied in the room. The smell aroused Billy and he was ready for another round but Karen knew they had things to do that day.

After a quick shower together that included some more intimacy, they dressed and went down to the coffee shop for some breakfast. Karen ordered a short-stack with bacon, Billy chose a lighter fare…Special K with bananas and an English Muffin.

Billy watched the young girl tackle the pancakes which she drowned in maple syrup. She took a breath to look up at Billy who had a broad grin on his face. "What's so funny?" she asked half-heartedly.

"I'm just enjoying watching you eat. Nothing more. Finish up because we have some important things to talk about and I need your total attention." She wiped the remnants of the syrup from her plate with the last pancake…took a sip of coffee and leaned back waiting for Billy to talk.

"I think you know that I didn't come back to Detroit to kill Sugar. I want to be totally honest with you before you put me on a pedestal. Someone very close to me was murdered. The shots that took her life were meant for me. She just got in the line of fire. She was carrying my child at the time."

"My God I'm so sorry Billy. I never knew you had a wife. Do you know who did this?"

"Yes I do. He lives in Bloomfield Hills. He is very wealthy and powerful with strong mob connections. I came back to kill him."

Karen listened carefully as he spoke. "Billy why not just go to the police? Tell them who did it and let them arrest the guy."

"I wish it was that simple Karen. He was not the one that pulled the trigger but he hired the assassins. Of that I have no doubt. But I have no proof that I can take to the authorities. They won't arrest someone on the word of a Cherokee from Oklahoma."

"So if this guy is so powerful and connected how are you going to get to him? Do you have a plan Billy?"

"I do but I can't do it alone. I need your help Karen. It's asking a lot and it might be dangerous for you. I need you to become a distraction that opens a window for me to do what I have to do."

"What kind of distraction?" she asked. At least she didn't say no until she heard him out.

Billy went on to describe Califano's habits and use of a driver and limo to take him home every night he was in town. "I need you to get the driver away from the car for two minutes…that's it. You are a beautiful girl, Karen and in the right outfit with a little makeup I think you can lure any man into your lair. You can tell him you think someone was following you or something like that."

Karen nodded her head. "I can do that. But what are you going to do with his limo? Please tell me you aren't going to use a bomb to kill him. Billy a lot of innocent people could get killed or crippled needlessly."

She was right and Billy had wrestled with that possibility ever since he came up with his plan. "Karen the bomb I made is very small with a very small amount of C-4. I used similar size charges in Vietnam with minimal collateral damage. I am pretty sure the only casualties will be the occupants."

"Pretty sure isn't good enough for me Billy. Sorry but I won't help you if there is any chance at all of an observer getting maimed or killed. There has to be another way."

Billy explained how he re-conned Califano's estate and the security obstacles that would prevent a head on assault. "I've wracked my brain trying to come up with another option. There is none and my guess he will heading out of town in a few days and I will lose my chance."

Karen thought for a moment, then made a suggestion. "I'll kill him."

* * *

After Karen outlined her plan, Billy agreed it had a good chance of working…and getting her killed in the process. "Have you every shot a gun, Karen? Have you ever killed anything? Taking a life is something that will find a dark, deep, hole in your soul that you can never remove…ever."

"Billy I owe you this. I can do this. I can get closer to this guy than you or anyone else can unless he likes boys. How good of a shot do I have to be when I'm sitting on the guy's lap?"

And so it was decided to proceed with Karen's plan. Billy was not disregarding the bomb as an option but this was a last resort if all else failed.

Karen spent most of the day picking an outfit from her new clothes that was seductive enough to set the trap. She settled on a very short black strapless dress with an ample view of her perky but small breasts. The push-up bra made them look larger than they were and the right amount of make-up completed the package. Once the clothing was nailed down, she had to get familiar with a 2 ½ pound Colt .45.

Karen stood in front of the mirror in their room and practiced pulling the heavy weapon from her purse and finding the safety. Over and over she practiced the draw, then she dry fired the Colt again and again, getting comfortable with the light trigger pull the gun was famous for. Billy wished he had time to take her to a gun range because the kick would certainly surprise her and affect the accuracy of a second shot if it was needed.

Billy wanted to be in position in front of the Renaissance Center by 5:30 to allow for an earlier than expected departure by Califano. He tried to give Karen an accurate description of his face and worried that she might not recognize him in time to act.

At four o'clock Billy told Karen to get ready. While she dressed, he checked that the Colt was clean, lubed and a full clip was loaded with hollow points. He decided to drop her off in front of the hotel entrance and then park nearby where he could see everything as it went down. Once the limo arrived, Billy would signal to Karen to watch for Califano to exit his tower. After that it was all up to her.

If she was able to get into the limo with Califano, she would shoot him in the head before they pulled away from the curb. She would jump from the car and Billy would pick her up and drive off before anyone could react. If he wouldn't invite her to enter the limo, she would shoot him from the curb and run south where Billy would be waiting. The wild card would be the driver. How he reacted could doom the plan before they could get away.

They couldn't leave the driver to chance. Billy would take him out with the AR-15 from his car if he could get a clear shot. The plan was messy as hell and if Karen was not in the loop Billy's homemade bomb would have been used.

* * *

The traffic into downtown was light as expected at 5:30. Most commuters were leaving the city, not coming in, and there were no sporting events that would have changed that dynamic. Billy pulled up to the curb in front of the main hotel entrance to let Karen out. She took one last look at herself in the visor mirror and turned to Billy. "Do I look like a seductive woman of the night?" Billy answered by giving her a final kiss on the cheek. "Be careful."

Karen had gone over the plan in her head a hundred times. Now it was show time and her knees were about to buckle…she was incredibly nervous as one would expect. She found a spot under an ornamental shade tree that gave her a sight line to Billy who had his binoculars trained on the exit Califano would use in less than an hour.

Ten minutes later the script changed. The black limo rolled up to the same spot it used every evening. Billy could see the silhouette of the driver as he lit a cigarette and lowered the driver side window to keep the smoke away from where his boss would sit.

Billy gave Karen the first signal, hitting the horn three times in quick succession. She pulled out her compact mirror for one final inspection then started to walk seductively to the tower entrance where the limo was stationed. Billy watched as she moved to the designated spot and lit a cigarette, letting the smoke drift slowly from her nostrils which caught the attention of every red blooded male within 20 yards. She was the flame and all the moths were moving in.

Any minute Califano would be coming out so Billy pulled the AR-15 from the floor and aimed it out the open window, draping it with his jacket to hide the barrel. He wished he had picked up a scope and suppressor but he was a sharpshooter with iron sights so he expected to hit his target with precision. The driver's head filled the sight window. He was about to die.

Five minutes later a tall man in dark suit came out of the tower entrance and headed to the waiting car. Seconds later Billy could see the man's face. It was Califano. Billy hit the horn three more times and Karen stepped forward, standing in the direct path of Califano who immediately noticed the hot girl who smiled at him as he got closer.

Califano stopped in front of Karen and began to say something but before he could form his words he saw the girl's hand rise from her large purse and aim the .45 at his head. A second later two shots rang out. The first came from Billy's carbine, shattering the glass of the limo and entering the driver's skull a quarter of an each behind his ear. He died instantly.

The second shot came from the heavy pistol Karen was pointing. She hesitated a fraction of a second to release the safety then fired. Her first shot was wild and missed Califano entirely, allowing him to dive into the open rear door. He saw his dead driver and pushed the body aside, allowing him room to climb over the seat to the driver's position. As he reached for the key, Karen moved to the driver's side and aimed again at her target. Before she could take the shot another explosion erupted, hitting Califano in the throat. The wound was not fatal but the blood gushing from his neck was a pretty good sign he was not long for this world.

Billy hit the horn three more times, then gunned the Olds to life and sped to where Karen was still standing, now surrounded by a growing crowd of witnesses. She was frozen, looking down at Califano as the gurgling sounds from his mouth grew softer. She knew he was still alive and also knew the job had to be finished. She aimed the Colt at his head and fired the kill shot. Billy pulled up and she jumped in next to him, still holding her weapon at her side.

Billy pushed her to the floor and the sped off towards the freeway out of the city. He got as far as 8-mile road before the radio reported the shooting at the Renaissance Center. She sat up next to him and she was shaking uncontrollably, forcing Billy to pull to the shoulder and comfort her. "I will never be able to thank you enough

Karen. My dead wife and child are watching and smiling down at this very moment. It's over."

CHAPTER 20

The parking lot at Ted's was almost full when Billy pulled in. Karen had calmed down enough to talk about what had just happened and she was not ashamed. In fact, she was proud that she could repay Billy for saving her life. Billy put his jacket over her exposed shoulders and she stopped shivering in the cold night air.

Neither of them had much of an appetite so he ordered milk shakes which would have to hold them over until they got back to the Ramada. "We need to ditch this car Karen. I'm sure a lot of people saw me pull away and may have even gotten the license plate number. I need you to call Gloria to pick us up here and drive us back. If she's the friend she claims she is I'm certain she won't refuse you."

Karen left the car and walked to the restaurant lobby where a couple of pay phones were not in use. Billy watched her as she walked. My God she was a sexy woman, he thought and there were plenty of other people making that same observation. Ten minutes later she was back in the car. "She's on her way."

It took almost an hour for Gloria to get to the drive-in. As she cruised through the parked cars, a horn blared out and she saw Karen waving at her. Fortunately, the spot next to Billy's rental was vacant and Gloria backed in. Karen jumped out first and climbed in to Gloria's front seat and hugged her. "Thank you so much. It's been a crazy day and my head is still spinning."

Billy opened the trunk of the Olds and pulled out the AR which was wrapped again in newspaper. He tapped on the window and Gloria opened the trunk of the Mustang. After tossing in the package, Billy climbed in next to Karen and Gloria drove off.

Before either passenger spoke, Gloria laid out the ground rules. "I don't want to know what you two have been up to. Don't tell me anything please."

Billy respected Gloria's demand. It was good strategy for all concerned. "OK, but I need to lose the package I put in your trunk. If there is a lake nearby we need to pay it a visit."

Instead of going south on Woodward, she drove west on Square Lake Road, past Telegraph to an area populated with several man-made lakes. The one nearest the road was Turtle Lake. There were only a few homes surrounding the lake, all of which were mansions with private roads, some of which were secured with steel fences and locked gates.

Gloria turned down a dirt road leading to the lake and stopped fifty yards from the shore line. "This is close enough. Turn off your headlights. I'll be right back." Gloria opened the trunk and Billy retrieved the rifle and jogged into the darkness. When he returned, he was unarmed. Both the rifle and his 1911 Colt were sitting at the bottom of Turtle Lake along with the improvised IED.

The drive back to the Ramada was awkward for all of them. Small talk was not Billy's specialty. Karen made several attempts to pick a topic that was not related to what had happened but Gloria would not respond until she pulled into the Ramada parking lot. "Look you two. Some pretty heavy shit went down today and I'm not stupid. Karen, I know you feel something strong and deep towards Mister Rambo here but he is a dangerous man. In the short time I've known you, Billy, a lot of people have died…many I know deserved what they got but no one is above the law and I can't accept what you did, no matter how honorable the motive."

Neither Billy nor Karen had anything to say. They got out of the car and headed to their room while Gloria returned to her job in the bar. They would never see each other again.

* * *

The NBC affiliate in Detroit was the first to break the news nationally on the bloody shoot-out in the posh Ren Cen area. Hours later it was the lead story on all the networks and CNN as well. The report had enough details to pique viewer interest in every area of the country. *'Vincent Califano, a prominent business man and his driver were gunned down as they were leaving their posh Renaissance Center Tower office for the day. Witnesses said the shooter was a tall woman in a black dress. Some reported that other shots were heard coming from a nearby parking lot but police have not confirmed that report. A sketch of the woman will be released to the public later this week.'*

Salvatore Bellante got word of Califano's death from the television before he got a call from his people on the ground. "What the fuck just happened?" he screamed to his consiglieri and two of his lieutenants who were sipping Espresso. "Califano wasn't the type to have some bimbo stashed away, was he? Jimmy, get on a plane and dig into this. Until you hear otherwise, you will be running the Detroit operations. Capisce?" James 'Squeaky' Gallanto was Sal's most trusted soldier. He had a brain as well as the balls needed to get things done.

At the same time Bellante was learning of the death of his man in Detroit, Wilson Whitehorse was getting a welcomed call from his son. "I saw the news Billy. Thank God you are OK. I hope you can find peace again. Come home, son."

"So now what?" Karen asked as she finished her breakfast. Billy was sitting across from her lost in thought. "Billy, did you hear me?" she asked again.

"Sorry," Billy answered as he tuned back in to their conversation. "Well I'm heading back to Oklahoma. My tribe needs me."

"I need you too Billy. Are you just going to toss me to the curb?" In her heart Karen knew he would never abandon her but becoming part of his real life was hard for her to digest.

"I think you already know the answer to that question, Karen. I would love for you to come with me but you have to want that as the next page in your life. My people have very strong traditions that go back hundreds of years, long before the white man set foot on our shores. You will be entering a whole new world but you will be welcomed like a part of our family. It's your choice."

* * *

The flight from Detroit was surprisingly right on time. Wilson and two of the tribal elders were waiting in baggage claim for the returning hero, eerily similar to Billy's return from Vietnam. What Billy did in Detroit would not get him any awards or medals but the Red Bison Clan was more proud of him than the country was those many years ago.

Billy waved when he saw his father and they shared an uncharacteristic but sincere hug. Stepping from behind stood a cute young girl. "Father, this is Karen. I owe her a lot and she will be part of our family for a while…for as long as she wants. I'll fill in the blanks on the drive home."

Without waiting for a response, Karen ran up and hug Billy's father. "I'm really honored to be here with Billy. I promise not to be a distraction." From that moment, she had Wilson Whitehorse in her pocket.

They arrived at the reservation to what might be called a Cherokee ticker tape parade. A row of pickups had children standing in the truck beds waving homemade signs that read *'We love you Billy!'* Rows of picnic tables were lined up in the baseball field and brisket was being carved for all the hungry well-wishers. There was another table covered with tubs of iced beer, mostly Budweiser…Billy's favorite.

A neighbor took Billy and Karen's luggage to Eva's old house and the returning couple helped themselves to all the good food that was prepared in their honor. Once everyone had filled their plates, Wilson rapped his fork against his beer bottle to get the crowd's attention.

"Thank you all for the warm greeting you have given my son and his new friend Karen. Future clan members will tell their grandchildren the story of how Billy Whitehorse brought honor and justice to our family. So much of our heritage has been ground into the dust of history by the white man. This story will survive and be told for a thousand years."

After the meal and much drinking, Billy and the remaining party goers were entertained by a group of young dancers in ceremonial costumes. This was Karen's first exposure to native American culture and she was overwhelmed by the beauty of the performance. "My God Billy you have so much to be thankful for. I am so happy to be welcomed in this way."

With the fire dying and most of the crowd dispersed back to their homes, Billy led Karen to the home of his dead love. It was a difficult trip for him to make...especially with another woman he was falling in love with.

The following morning, Karen was led off by several of the younger girls of the tribe for a kind of orientation and Billy met his father in the tribe's office. "Billy, I have good news. While you were dealing with Califano, Aubrey Bennison reached out to Shan Williams with an investment offer…a sizeable offer."

"I don't get it. Bennison is a billionaire with some of the largest and most successful casinos in Vegas and around the world. Why would he want to waste his time and money on a little Indian venture in Laughlin…a little off the beaten path from Sin City?"

"He wants to humiliate Damon Drummond…pure and simple. He hates him. Drummond tried to stiff him on a $10 million loan. If his father hadn't have died, he would have gone through a bankruptcy filing on the Palace and walked away neat and clean with Bennison holding the bag."

"Sounds great but we haven't even broken ground yet. How does investing in the future hurt Drummond now?"

"First things first. Shan wants to have a meeting as soon as possible to review Bennison's offer which he says is very strong and more than fair. I have us booked on a flight to Las Vegas tomorrow afternoon. There are no direct flights into Laughlin so Shan will drive in to meet us. Bennison has offered us a suite at The Sands, one of his properties on the Strip."

"Sounds good. That will give me a chance to sit down with Willy and the band and let them know I will not be staying on. Have to say I really miss performing. Playing guitar got me through some pretty dark times after the war ended." Billy had never talked to his father about those dark times and Wilson's heart broke when he heard those words.

CHAPTER 21

"We are ahead of schedule and under budget…amazing!" Jill Beauville was going over the most recent update on the Palace renovations with Damon. Being the cautious conservative manager that Damon wasn't, she took great pride in this revelation.

With the Miss USA Pageant officials coming in for a final walk-thru, this was very good news. More recent good news was Elena's announcement that she was pregnant with their second child…hopefully a brother to Nicole who was growing like a weed.

"We are only three weeks away from the pageant and I haven't met any of the contestants yet. Jill, get them in here asap, please. Fly them in on the Drummond jet and get them rooms at the Palace for a couple of nights. I'll personally accompany them from McCarran to the Palace."

Although there were fifty girls representing every part of the country, they all were in New York getting fitted for the gowns and bathing suits they would be wearing when the competition began. "We can't get them all in here three weeks early. They have contractual obligations to the sponsors. You'll just have to wait til they arrive the week of the pageant." Jill loved busting Damon's balloon.

Damon wouldn't give up. "Get me pictures of all the girls. I'll pick a couple to bring in for promotional photos or whatever. Just get me something now."

Jill knew where this was going. Damon was not one to appreciate the beauty of budding motherhood and as Elena grew larger he avoided intimate contact with his wife all together. His roving eye was well known within the Palace staff but he was cautious in keeping his dalliances away from Laughlin. The thought of cornering some beauty pageant contestants was too much for his libido to deal with. He was licking his lips.

The following morning Damon was looking at glossy's of six gorgeous women. One in particular leaped out at him…Miss Arizona. Her bio read that she was a student at Arizona State; stood 5'9"; long blonde hair and, most important to Damon, a generous bust line. He picked out two other blondes and ordered Jill to get those three girls in to Vegas by weeks' end.

At the last minute, Damon decided to personally fly to New York and escort the girls back to Vegas. He left instructions for Jill to hire a photographer and arrange a photo shoot. She knew the pictures would never be seen.

* * *

It was a short cab ride to the Sands from the airport and Billy and Wilson were greeted by a lovely fruit and cheese basket in their two-bedroom suite. At check-in, they were told that the hotel had comped $1,000 each in chips that they could use as they please…compliments of Aubrey Bennison.

Shan was due to arrive in the morning which gave Billy a chance to retrieve his car and meet with his old bandmates. "I'm going out to clean up some loose ends Pop. Have fun in the casino and try not to lose all your money in the first hour. I may be out late but I'll try not to wake you when I get in."

Billy walked to his apartment and found everything exactly as he had left it. He had few possessions other than his clothes and guitar rig and it didn't take long to fill up his old army duffle bag. The music gear was still at the last gig so all he had to take with him was his trusty Gibson. He threw the luggage in the trunk of his Trans Am and prayed that it would start which it did on the first try.

It was almost 8 pm and he figured the band was doing a sound-check at this time. He drove to the Stardust and valet parked, removing his duffle and guitar which he carried in to the concierge station. "Hey Phil, can I leave this stuff here for a minute while I talk to Willy?"

The bell captain was a wannabe rock star and always sat in awe of Billy as he shredded powerful solos night after night. "No problem Billy. You back with the band now?"

Billy walked across the casino floor and found the band almost ready for the first set downbeat. When they saw Billy, the players all embraced him like a lost son. "Man it's good to see you brother." Willy was more than ready to have his old guitarist back. "When did you get in?"

"I just got in today. Staying at the Sands with my father. We have a business meeting in the morning. I'm afraid I will be moving permanently back to Tulsa. My family needs me and I've had a family death to deal with since you last saw me. I hope you understand."

"Man that is bad news amigo. We're all gonna miss you my brother. You want to sit in for a couple of tunes…for old times?"

Billy immediately accepted and asked his replacement if he could use his guitar. The next thirty minutes was a master class on blues guitar and the crowd that was streaming in showed their appreciation with hearty applause. When he was finished he walked to the bar with Willy Deville and handed him the keys to his Trans Am. "I want you to have my ride. Drive it or sell it…whatever you want. You've been a real friend and probably saved my life when you hired me to play with you." The two musicians hugged each other and Billy walked to retrieve his luggage.

As Billy stood at the bell stand, a large white stretch limo pulled up. Loud disco music was streaming from the speakers as the occupants climbed out, spilling champagne in the process. Billy watched and was stunned at the beauty of the young girls that he saw. They stood and waited as the last rider climbed out…Damon Drummond.

It took Billy a moment to recognize the tall man with the blonde hair. He had never met Drummond but saw his photo in several tabloids showing him partying all over the Strip. The entourage entered the casino oblivious to those staring at them. They headed to the lounge where Willy was playing and the party sped up to warp speed.

Billy was surprised to find his father still up and watching a movie when he returned. "Hey Pop, you will never guess who I ran into at the Stardust…Damon Drummond. He was with a bunch of very hot girls parading around like they were celebrities. The arrogant little shit will be surprised when we open our casino in his back yard."

The next morning Wilson got a call from Aubrey Bennison. "Welcome to my town Mister Whitehorse. I hope you and your son find everything to your satisfaction. I'm calling from my office in the Sands Convention center. Mister Williams has already arrived and is sitting across from me." He put the call on speaker phone for Williams.

"Hi Wilson and Billy. Aubrey is having breakfast brought in so get over here as soon as you can." Aubrey jumped in…"There is a car waiting for you at the main entrance."

Twenty minutes later they were all sitting at a large 18th Century conference table covered with assorted pastries and glasses of cold orange and grapefruit juice. A large sterling silver carafe with hot coffee was brought in after they were all seated. The server filled each man's cup and then excused himself.

Bennison started the meeting. "Gentlemen I think we all know why we are here this morning. I have a very strong interest in investing in the construction and operation of the new casino and resort you are planning on tribal land in Laughlin."

Billy jumped right in with the obvious first question. "Mister Bennison, you have punched all the buttons in the gaming industry already. You have some of the largest and most lavish operations on three continents that I am aware of. Why Laughlin and why us?"

"First, please call me Aubrey. Now, you ask a very logical question and I want to answer you honestly. I like Laughlin because it does not represent a direct conflict with my Vegas enterprises. I would never risk taking jobs from my existing employees just to get a little richer. Also, your project already has a prime location that, if done right, will pull business from Phoenix, Denver and other adjacent markets. And finally, I want to destroy Damon Drummond. I have personal reasons that I won't go into now but, seeing the Palace fail will give me great pleasure."

Shan was next to weigh in. "Your reasons make sense Aubrey and your reputation is well known and respected. It is obvious that you understand the financial need of our group. We have met with several potential investors. Some proved to have motives that are not in keeping with our culture and laws. The others were not willing to come to the table with the funds necessary to strike a deal. Despite these setbacks, we are not going to charge into an agreement that is not thoroughly vetted."

"Understood." Aubrey answered. "Shan, my sources tell me you guys need around $10 million to get this thing built. I'm willing to provide that funding. In return, I have very simple and fair demands. First, I want the new hotel to be larger, taller and more luxurious than the Palace. I won't ask for veto power over the decisions on how it is decorated or laid out. That is totally your call. Second, I want the Marina to be state of the art in every respect. If that requires going over budget I will cover it. I will be keeping one of my luxury yachts there. It will be a drawing card to others with sizeable boats in the area. Finally, I want forty percent ownership which gets you access to my years of experience in building and managing a resort casino."

Billy was about of reply but Wilson motioned him to silence. "Aubrey, your proposal is fair and reasonable but Shan and I have others that must be given a chance to weigh in. That may take a few days. Is that acceptable?"

"It is but I do have a timetable that must be met. I want to have a ground breaking ceremony at the same time that the Miss USA pageant is kicked off in two weeks. I will need a little time to get the press on board and I want to bring in some star power…major star power."

"Very well. Either Shan or I will get back to you within 48 hours with our decision. I assume you can have the necessary documents drawn up by your attorneys." They exchanged handshakes and filed out of the meeting room. “Looks like we have a new casino to build,” Wilson announced as they rode back to the Sands.

CHAPTER 22

Elena stared at the brown envelope for a long time, afraid to open it. The sender was anonymous. Reluctantly, she slid the opener along the edge and pulled out a series of photos. Each picture was worse than the one before it. Damon was shown cavorting with several alleged contestants to the Miss USA Pageant in a lounge at the Stardust. The next few showed him kissing and fondling the breasts of one of the girls in the back of his limo. The final picture showed the girl's dress up and Damon's hands on her panties touching her vagina.

She had no illusions about Damon's fidelity. She accepted his affairs as long as he never embarrassed her and kept everything under wraps. This time he went too far and she would make him pay. She sent the photos and the pre-nup she had signed to her attorney to see what her options might be. She wanted to take him to the cleaners but she also had a new baby to think about. The attorney advised two things…say nothing to anyone about what she had until she delivered the baby. Then demand a ridiculous amount and watch him squirm.

As hard as it would be, she would bide her time as her attorney instructed. It wouldn't be difficult, as her husband was engrossed in getting the Miss USA Pageant off the ground and was never home. The pre-nup had an escape clause if it could be proven that one of the partners had an affair or casual sex with another person. Elena's attorney would put an investigator on Damon to get the proof they would need. If successful, Elena would walk away with millions that would set her and her children up for life. She would never find out that it was Jill Beauville who sent the pictures.

* * *

After a brief conference call with both tribe's elders, it was decided to accept Bennison's offer. The architect began working on revising the initial plans to achieve the goals of their new partner. Bennison wired the contract to Shan who signed on behalf of both tribes.

Wilson and Shan agreed that someone should devote 100% of their time overseeing the project on site. Shan didn't have the time to make that commitment and Wilson didn't have the stamina. Billy ended up drawing the short straw.

"I would be honored to manage the project, father, as long as both tribes agree to give me wide latitude in moving things along. I want to earn the respect of the contractors and workers and to do so, we need to treat them fairly and with respect."

The groundbreaking ceremony was scheduled to coincide with the first day of the Miss USA Pageant at the Palace. Bennison sent out his invitations and the response was overwhelming. The guests included First Lady Hillary Clinton, Nevada Governor Bob Miller, Senator Ben Nighthorse Campbell of Colorado and a slew of celebrities currently performing on The Strip. Billy, Shan and Wilson would do the honors with gold plated shovels.

Billy was eager to move to the Laughlin reservation, his home for the duration of the construction project, and hoped that Karen would join him. She had settled nicely into the Red Bison family and was learning the ropes of managing Eva's shop.

"How long will we be gone?" Karen asked when Billy laid out the relocation plan. "I'm starting to get the shop back on its feet and I love being needed and contributing to the community."

"Conservative estimates are 18 months for the hotel and casino and another 6 months for the marina and camp grounds." Billy was being optimistic and did not mention setbacks that would surely pop up along the way.

"I can't imagine being away from you for a year and a half, Billy. But I don't want to abandon the shop and all the work I've put into making it profitable again. I'm so sorry but you brought me here and it has changed my life. If you care for me, you will not make me choose."

Billy had no good argument to make. She was right. She was thriving among his people and the scars from her past were healing. "You're right Karen. I will miss you more than you can imagine but it's not the end of the world. I'll be coming back from time to time and maybe I can steal you away for a few days to join me as well."

A few days later, Billy was back on a plane to Las Vegas where he found a two-year-old F-150 waiting for him, courtesy of the Fort Mohave Tribe. It would be his for the duration of his stay.

* * *

Damon was still not fully awake. He took in the naked beauty lying next to him and watched her breasts rise and fall with each breath. No need to wake her, he decided, as he put on his robe before retrieving the newspapers that were slid under the door to his suite.

He called down for coffee and a few pastries and when they arrived he settled in to read the paper. Both the

Sun and the Review-Journal had front page articles announcing the ground breaking ceremony for the new Indian owned casino in Laughlin. A picture of Aubrey Bennison shaking hands with his two tribal partners filled most of the page. As re read through the article, the date for the official groundbreaking jumped off the page. "That mother fucker!" Damon screamed, waking up Miss Arizona in the process.

"Is something wrong, Damon?" the tall blonde asked as she wrapped her arms around her new friend. She was still naked and he could feel her breasts against his back which immediately took his attention away from the headlines he was reading.

"Later dammit!" he shouted at the young girl who left him to his papers and headed to the shower. He picked up the phone and called Jill. "Did you see the papers this morning? That cock sucker is trying to ruin the pageant…and me!"

Jill had already seen the news and was expecting Damon's frantic call. "Settle down, Damon. It's just a ground breaking ceremony. We'll be getting all the real attention. Their event will be over in a few minutes and then the focus will shift to us. Remember, we have Dick Clark." What she didn't mention was the list of guests that were not in the initial newspaper reports. She knew that when he found out, he would go ballistic.

The week of the pageant and the ground breaking were a swirl of activity in both camps. The pageant contestants arrived and were covered with photo ops up and down the strip. Damon was front and center for most of them and was begging high profile performers to attend the pageant. It was then that he learned the bad news…all the big names would be at the ground breaking if, for no other reason, than to rub elbows with the First Lady. Damon had nothing that could trump that star power. His best shot were judges Scott Baio from the cancelled 'Joanie Loves Chachi' television show and magician Lance Burton. Damon would be the final judge.

At his father's request, Billy cut off his long black hair which had never seen a pair of scissors since he returned from Vietnam. He was fitted, along with Wilson and Shan, for traditional black tuxedos which was Bennison's idea. Billy wanted to wear traditional Cherokee costumes but was overruled.

The Miss USA Pageant coverage was to go live on CBS at 7 pm. Once it was announced that Hillary Clinton would be at the ground breaking, all the networks, including CBS decided to cut away to see her appearance.

Bennison was in seventh heaven. When he was finished, the Drummond name and brand would be worthless.

Governor Miller and Senator Campbell were flown in ahead of Clinton and were on the tarmac with Bennison to meet Air Force One. Using the president's plane was highly unusual but with approval ratings going through the roof, no one would challenge her use of the plane.

Bennison made sure all of the local network affiliates were there to cover the landing and greeting on the red carpet. A microphone was set up for the First Lady to make a few comments and take a couple of questions from the press and she performed perfectly.

"I want to thank Governor Miller, Senator Campbell and representatives from the Fort Mohave and Red Bison tribes for inviting me to this historical event. The Indian Gaming Regulatory Act was designed to open opportunities to Native Americans in the lucrative gaming industry. The ground breaking ceremony tonight celebrates this important breakthrough and is long overdue. I also want to thank Aubrey Bennison for his participation in this project. He brings years of expertise that will insure the new casino is a resounding success."

The motorcade headed out for the drive to Laughlin with a police escort leading the way. Damon watched it all in his suite, now accompanied by his pregnant wife and child. Elena could barely contain her glee as she watched Damon boil over. "You need to get ready, Damon. We'll be watching here in the room." She had no intention of being a partner in his humiliation.

Damon took one last look at himself in the mirror before going down to meet the press and Dick Clark. He looked pretty dashing in his white dinner jacket and a can of Aqua Net insured every blonde hair was firmly in place.

Jill was waiting for him and they walked together to the center of the lobby where the cameras were set up. After greeting the pageant officials, Damon took his seat with the other judges and waited for Dick Clark to get things started.

Just as Clark was welcoming the home audience; he was interrupted by sirens and flashing lights. The Clinton motorcade was passing slowly by the Palace and drew all the pageant on-lookers to the street to wave at the First Lady. The press immediately followed and took pictures for their morning editions.

Clark did his best to kill time until the motorcade passed and decided to introduce Damon first and then the other judges. Damon made a feeble attempt to hype the size of the crowd and the drama of what was to follow. He failed miserably. His night was over before it began and Elena could see it in his face on the television screen. She had absolutely zero sympathy for him.

CHAPTER 23

For three months after the pageant, Damon was deluged with bad press while the new casino's construction became the symbol of the future of Nevada's primary industry. Bennison used his considerable influence and resources to sustain the enthusiasm, and decided to have a contest to name the new Resort and Casino complex. Wilson and Shan were against the idea as was Billy. They wanted a name that honored their culture but couldn't agree on what that should be.

To compromise, Bennison suggested they provide three or four names and then let the public choose from those. After much debate, they came to agreement to proceed with the contest. They chose three names… "Mystic River Resort and Casino"; "Three Corners Resort and Casino"; "Moon Shadow Resort and Casino".

The naming contest was a local event but immediately drew national attention, partly due to the fact that it was a Native American project but mostly because of quid pro quo manipulations by the Bennison empire with the national television networks.

As Bennison and the tribes basked in the spotlight, Damon Drummond watched the Palace descend into near insolvency. His signature enterprise was bleeding and it was a wound that may prove fatal if it continued. He became increasingly less visible to the public and even the executives within his own organization. He would occasionally sneak out at night alone and visit the new casino construction site. What he saw only increased his depression and sense of pending failure.

Even the birth of his son provided little reason to smile. Elena was different and he sensed she was becoming more independent and less susceptible to his relentless bullying. After the baby's baptism, she dropped the bomb. The divorce papers cited numerous acts of infidelity by her husband, supported by video and photo documentation. Without the protection of the pre-nup, Damon stood to lose half of everything he owned.

Forced to move out of the penthouse, Damon took a lower level suite but spent most of his time at his Vegas corporate office. He adopted a bunker mentality with few sympathizers in his inner circle. A stream of resignations soon followed the news of the divorce announcement and the pending death of the Palace was becoming an anchor, likely to drag down the entire Drummond conglomerate.

* * *

Jackie Zerilli was an admirer of Aubrey Bennison. In fact, he was almost jealous of the success Bennison achieved largely within the law. The fact that he got in bed with the very operation that Bellante and Califano failed to lock down just added to his infatuation with the gaming kingpin.

The newly named Mystic River Resort and Casino was into the final stage of construction and Zerilli was well aware of the impact the changing landscape in Laughlin was having on the Drummond Palace. Bellante was never able to find whoever it was that took out Califano but all fingers seemed to point towards the man whose wife took the hit meant for him. His name was Billy Whitehorse and he was now the point man for the tribe at the construction site. Zerilli was reading the tea leaves and he was becoming convinced an opportunity was laying at his feet. Time for a meeting with Damon Drummond.

* * *

"Who is this guy?" Damon asked Jill when the phone message was handed to him. Jill immediately recognized the name and shuddered at what it could mean for their future.

"Jackie Zerilli is a mobster, Damon. His family has their fingers in lots of things, some legitimate but most operating under the radar of the law. Do you want to call him back?"

"Sure. Let's find out what's on his mind." Damon was looking for a life raft and didn't really care who was throwing it to him.

Zerilli was an avid golfer and worked out of a bungalow on the grounds of the Desert Inn Golf Club. Although he was a young man, he hated the noise of the big Strip casinos, especially the ones that catered to families with screaming kids. At the Desert Inn, he could walk out his door and be standing on the 5th tee.

When Drummond's call came in he extended an invitation for a round of golf and it was immediately accepted. Damon arrived on time, rare for him, and was left cooling his heels at the first tee while other foursomes went ahead of him. After almost an hour, Zerilli rolled up in his custom-made golf cart and waved Damon over.

"Welcome to my Palace. Not quite on the scale of your place but I like the coziness here. I guess by now you did your homework and know who I am and what I do. Let's get started and we can talk while we play." Damon threw his clubs in Jackie's cart and they each teed off. Just the two of them.

Zerilli's cart was well stocked with beer and pre-mixed margaritas and by the third tee, Damon was feeling loose and eager to talk. "Look Jackie, I get what's going on here. Why not just lay your cards on the table?"

"Sure, no problem." Jackie pulled the car off the path under a beautiful cypress tree and popped open another Rolling Rock. "Look, you and I, we're both business men. The difference is I know what the fuck I'm doing and you are a bozo. I know that hurts and pisses you off but it's time for a reality check little buddy. You're getting slapped around like a cheap piñata. Everything in your life has turned to shit…your marriage, your business…everything."

"Fuck you!" Damon hissed. "What gives you the right to judge me?"

"Relax, I'm just pointing out the obvious, OK? I asked you here to offer you a way out of the shit storm you created. I have a bone to pick with those Indian fucks that are building that new casino that is giving you agita. My reasons are none of your business so don't ask."

"So you want to help me to get revenge for something you won't tell me about? I think you're out of your fucking mind. Don't worry, I'll get through this without any help from people like you. I know all about you."

Jackie was losing his patience. "You better think long and hard my friend. I will make this offer only once. I can make the Indians go away and I can get your wife off your back…easy-peasy. Should I continue?"

Damon liked what he was hearing but knew that kind of help comes with a high price. "OK, I'm listening."

"Good. For my generous assistance, I get 51% of the Palace and 30% of the rest of your holdings. This is not negotiable. When the shit starts flying you have my guaranty none of it will hit you."

Damon was shocked at how much he was being asked to give up. "And if I decline your generosity?"

"Really? Well, for starters I buy the Palace out of bankruptcy for ten cents on the dollar. Anything with your name on it gets sent to the homeless in Somalia. Then I'll watch as your wife rips your heart out and you end up with nothing but debt and when your loans are called in I'll pick whatever meat is left off your bones. Look at the bright side. Maybe your wife will remarry someone who adopts your kids. When you die the Drummond name dies with you…in disgrace. Heads I win, tails I win."

Damon let Jackie's words sink in. He knew he really had no choice if he hoped to save his crumbling empire. "If I agree to this, I don't want to know anything about how you go about taking down the Indians. My name never gets mentioned or linked in any way. I'll sign over the 51% of the Palace now but nothing more until I see results."

"Listen, Damon. I can't guaranty you won't get a little dirt on your lily-white hands. Comes with the territory. If I have to wait on the 30% of the other holdings, the price goes to 40%...take it or leave it. Do we have a deal?" Damon shook his hand. He was about to dance with the devil.

* * *

Billy was tired and lonely. Construction was moving ahead on schedule and he had made many new friends within the Fort Mohave Tribe. Still he missed Karen so much he began to drink a little more than he should. Shan could see the change in his friend and suggested a visit to Las Vegas to see the band Redbone perform. The band was well known to Billy who always admired the fact that they were the first Native American rock band to have a certified number one hit...*Come and*

Get Your Love. In fact, Jimi Hendrix, part Cherokee himself, inspired the formation of the band back in 1969.

The concert was a good divergent for Billy. He even got to sit in on a couple of tunes, courtesy of Pat Vegas, lead singer and founding member. A highlight of their act was the bass player doing a ceremonial dance just prior to their performance. Billy and Shan were having a great time, as was another audience member…but he was watching Billy not the band.

Back on the job the following day, Billy decided he needed to see Karen now…not in ten days as was already planned. "Hey, I need to see you as soon as possible. I'm going nuts. Can you catch a flight tomorrow?" He left the message on her home answering machine and hoped she retrieved it quickly.

Most of the day was spent coordinating the carpet laying on the casino floor. Once that was completed, they could start rolling in the slots and gaming tables. Billy insisted that the carpet have an Indian theme and was very pleased with the final product. The carpet crew worked until 9 pm and Billy stayed until they were finished for the day.

The security guards from the Tribe were due to arrive at 10 pm so Billy took a seat on a roll of padding and smoked a cigarette. Billy never noticed the explosives planted throughout the casino and by the time he detected the faint almond smell, it was too late. The man sitting in the car could see the casino interior and Billy and pressed the button on his watch, detonating the first bomb which triggered the chain of explosives that buried Billy in rubble.

The fire department and ambulances arrived about thirty minutes after the explosion and Shan and the security team showed up shortly thereafter. Most of the fire was centered where the carpet and padding rolls were stored and was extinguished quickly. The casino floor was destroyed and the entire ceiling littered the area with glass and plaster.

The police tried to find out who was inside at the time of the blast and all of the workers were accounted for. When Shan realized that Billy was not among those, he ordered that dogs be brought in to sniff the debris in hopes of finding him. Despite their training, the canines were confused by the smell of the C-4 and it took more than two hours before a sustained bark identified the location of something or someone. It was Billy and he was still alive.

CHAPTER 24

Karen refused to leave his room at the Valley View Medical Center. Billy had been in a coma going on three days. His injuries were significant...broken collar bone, skull fracture and internal bleeding for starters. When Karen was notified of the explosion, she insisted on going with Wilson and they took the first available flight.

Shan had been meeting with the local police and a few days later, the FBI was brought in. The event was being described as a racist attack on a minority and the Nevada Attorney General insisted that the might of Washington weigh in with a complete team of investigators.

The insurance company wasted no time getting on the scene as well. Tribal construction was always self-insured but Bennison insisted that an outside company protect his sizeable investment. It would take at least a week to get an accurate assessment of the damage and only then could they look at rebuilding.

When the local station broke in with the news of the blast, Damon knew exactly who was responsible. He never expected anyone getting hurt and the man rescued from the rubble was barely alive. Still, the bright side was that his potential competitor was set back months, making the Palace the only game in town in Laughlin. Knowing Bennison was losing his ass made his day.

Damon waited for the call from Zerilli and it came in as expected. "So it looks like the Indians got their teepee trashed. You should be dancing in the street. If you have half a brain, and I'm not sure you do, you can turn this in to a windfall for your sinking Palace. Don't fuck this up because you're not working with house money…it's my money."

"No one was supposed to get hurt. Your people fucked up and now there is a witness that is alive in the hospital. If he saw anything before the explosion, we are screwed. You need to fix this before you get the rest of the pie." Damon talked tough but no one threatened Jackie Zerilli.

Jackie laughed at Damon's bravado. "Damon Drummond…so now you're a tough guy. I am really impressed. I want you to take a look at the picture of your kids you keep on your desk. Very cute…like their mother. If I hear any more shit coming out of your mouth, you'll never see those kids again…NEVER! I know a piece of shit like you probably doesn't give a fuck about your family but maybe I'm wrong."

"What about the guy in the hospital?" Damon needed to defuse the conversation.

"He's a dead man. Don't worry about it." Jackie knew the man in the hospital was Billy Whitehorse. He was supposed to die in the blast so finishing the job was always part of the script. "Now it's time to move on to your divorce settlement. I need you to give me the name of your wife's attorney. Remember you're not gonna get outta this clean so come up with a number you can live with and we'll make her an offer she can't refuse."

* * *

The Jennings and Kauffman law firm was one of the most effective and least known in Nevada. Specializing in family law, they built their reputation by getting divorce settlements that were beyond any expectations for their clients…and keeping the details out of the press. Michael Jennings got his start as part of the General Council team for Wilfred Drummond. His work on behalf of Drummond Construction was methodical and flawless and did not go unnoticed by the company's founder.

Michael was the same age as Wilfred's son Damon and was everything that Damon wasn't…discreet, loyal, and generous. In time Michael became more of a son than an employee which pissed off Damon more than his father ever knew. When Michael decided to accept a partner position in a new firm in Las Vegas, he left with the blessings of his benefactor.

When Damon chose to marry Elena, Wilfred hired Michael on a retainer basis to keep an eye on Damon and make sure his new wife didn't take his son to the cleaners. He ultimately designed the pre-nuptial agreement that was signed by the newlyweds. In the process, Michael and his wife Laura had social interactions with Damon and Elena and a friendship was formed between the two couples. After Damon made several unsuccessful passes at Michael's wife, Elena apologized to Michael and a real fondness developed between them.

When Wilfred died, Michael was free of any fiduciary responsibility to the Drummond companies. Still he continued the relationship with Damon and Elena, who was now becoming a kid sister to him, until Damon's infidelities surfaced. It was Michael whom Elena turned to to handle the divorce.

* * *

After cleaning up the Califano mess in Detroit, Jimmy Gallanto returned to Las Vegas and was elevated to a leadership position working directly for Jackie Zerilli. He was the one that was given the task of cleaning up the divorce problems for Damon Drummond.

The initial audit conducted by Jennings and Kauffman of Damon's net worth was $985 million. That number was now in free fall with the heavy losses that continued to decimate the company. Elena wanted half…all in cash. Damon wanted to settle for $25 million, retaining total ownership of all the real estate and corporate assets. It was now Gallanto's job to get her acceptance of the reduced offer.

"So Mister Gallanto, what firm do you represent? I don't believe I've seen you listed as a member of the Nevada bar." Michael took the meeting believing he would be sitting across from a legal representative for Damon Drummond.

Being articulate was not one of Jimmy's strengths. "I represent Mister Smith and Mister Wesson. Ever hear of them?" Michael was waiting for a smile to appear on his visitor's face but it never came.

"OK Mister Gallanto, I'm a busy man so get to the point please. Why are you here?" The slightest appearance of fear began to show in Michael's eyes and was not missed by Gallanto.

"I have a settlement offer from Mister Drummond. He wants this shit to go away. The offer is $25 million. Nothing more. Tell your client to take the offer and go on with her life. If she refuses this offer or goes to the press it will be rescinded and will be followed by unnecessary hardship for her and her kids." He slid a piece of paper with a phone number on it then stood to leave. Meeting over.

Michael had heard enough. "Are you threatening my client? Do you know the penalty for this kind of bullying? By the time you get to your car I'll have the authorities all over your ass."

Gallanto stopped and turned around. "Be careful when you turn out the lights tonight. You have as much to lose as your client. Have a nice day, and say hello to Laura for me."

Message received loud and clear. Michael would call Elena and advise her to take this offer.

* * *

Billy was alone in his room when he awoke from the coma. A passing nurse noticed him trying to get out of his bed and rushed in past the security guards and called for an on duty doctor. Bennison had agreed with Wilson that it would be a good idea to have protection for his son while he was in the hospital and two tribal college athletes volunteered for the assignment. Neither was armed but both were well skilled in martial arts and supremely confident they could repel anyone with bad intentions for Billy.

Later in the day the neurologist assigned to Billy made his evaluation that everything looked normal and Billy could begin physical therapy for his other injuries. Karen knew firsthand the benefits of PT and insisted on being an active observer and, if allowed, participant in Billy's prescribed program. "Well Geronimo, it looks like you are on the road to recovery."

"What the fuck happened?" Billy asked, still unaware of the details of the explosion. "I was sitting having a smoke when all hell came down on me."

"You were buried in debris but a rescue dog found you. He probably saved your life. You need to buy him a thick steak when you get out of here. There is no question that someone tried to sabotage the construction site. The police discovered the remains of four bombs. They won't say what they were made from but I'm sure they have a good idea if they were hi-tech or homemade."

Billy had a million questions. "Any idea who planted them and why? We can't afford for another attack to happen if we want to get this casino built in my lifetime…oops…bad joke I guess."

As the days passed, more information was released to Billy and his family. A dark colored SUV was seen parked in the construction site minutes before the explosion. The teenage couple that made the report were reluctant to come forward for obvious reasons but realized staying silent might lead to more incidents. They could not describe the occupant or occupants but felt sure the car was a Lincoln or Cadillac high end model.

As Billy improved and with his discharge date around the corner, his primary physical therapist failed to show up for his normal shift and a new face replaced him. Karen introduced herself and made small talk until Billy arrived, now using a walker rather than crutches or a wheel chair. The new guy was certainly fit and impressed Karen with his bulging muscles that almost ripped through his blue hospital sweats. What was also apparent to Karen and Billy was that the guy didn't know shit about the workout regimen that was developed for Billy.

"Hey buddy, are you trained for this kind of work?" Billy's internal alarms were starting to go off. He could see from Karen's face that she also was beginning to smell a rat and she excused herself, hoping she could get the attention of Billy's guards that were sitting down the hall.

"Yeah, I've been trained," the therapist answered and he began to move behind Billy who was lifting weights with leg stirrups. The large man reached down and lifted his pant leg, exposing a large hunting knife. As he began to pull it out, Karen screamed out Billy's name.

Billy reacted instinctively and dove to the floor as the knife was coming down to where he was sitting only seconds before. As Billy rolled away from his attacker, the two guards ran forward to grab the assailant's arms and received a slashing attack that left one of them with one arm spouting blood from a six-inch gash. The other guard wrestled to take the knife away but was physically smaller and unable to repel the attack.

The scuffle gave Billy enough time to get to his feet and pick up a 20-pound bar bell just as the attacker turned to finish the job. He was met by the weight slamming into the side of his head, crushing his skull and dropping him to the floor. Billy jumped on top of him and picked up the knife which he held against the man's throat. "Who sent you? Tell me and you might still survive. Who the fuck sent you?"

The attacker was barely conscious and was babbling something that was virtually inaudible. Billy bent down and put his ear up to the man's mouth and listened carefully. Seconds later a massive clot burst in his brain and he was dead.

At that moment, the PT ward was filled with medical staff tending to the wounds of the two fallen body guards, soon followed by the local police. Karen was helping Billy who was unhurt. "Why are they doing this to us?" she sobbed over and over. "Why Billy? Did he say anything to you before he died?"

Billy hugged her softly then whispered to her. "He said one word…Drummond."

CHAPTER 25

Zerilli's phone would not stop ringing with calls from Damon Drummond. After the fifth attempt to reach him Zerilli answered. "You are becoming a huge pain in the ass Damon. If you're calling to thank me for cleaning up your divorce mess don't bother. Just send over the papers giving me 40% of Drummond Construction and all the other Drummond holdings."

"I think I would rather talk about the new fuck-up of your team of clowns. The guy is in the hospital and he still manages to fuck you over. Please explain." Damon was showing remarkable self-control which was probably a good thing given who he was talking to.

"I'm going to ignore your tone one last time. For your information, I lost one of my best guys so excuse me for not really giving a fuck about your feelings."

"Listen to me Jackie. If that guy saw or knew anything that could hurt us, the feds would already be climbing up our asses. Forget about him. Everything we set out to do is done…finished. You kept your end of the deal and I will certainly keep mine. It's over."

"It's not over until I say it is. Taking out this Indian prick is personal for me. Understand? Just do what you do and stay out of my way." He hung up without another word. Two days later the Zerilli family was the proud owner of 40% of Drummond's financial life.

* * *

"The attacker had zero ID on him. We are running his prints now through the FBI data base but so far we haven't heard anything back." Billy had finished his interview but did not mention to the detective what the man said before he died. This was personal now and Billy would get his pound of flesh or die trying. First he needed to get back to 100% and then sit down with Aubrey Bennison…the only man that could supply the help Billy needed.

After being discharged from the hospital, Billy visited the young guards that were injured in the hospital attack. One was fully recovered from superficial knife wounds. The other was still hospitalized and may end up losing the use of his right arm. Billy promised to them that he would find who was behind the attack and that he would take care of whatever expenses the insurance or the tribe didn't cover.

Karen spent a week with him on the Fort Mohave Reservation but needed to get back to Oklahoma to tend to her shop. "I understand, Karen. I'll be fine so go home and take care of things. Once the construction crews finish the cleanup I will try to sneak back to see you for a few days. Wilson needs you too. I worry about the old guy and trust you will watch out for him."

Actually, Billy was anxious to get Karen out of town. With her around, he could not take the steps needed to satisfy his revenge. Watching her wave to him as she walked down the jetway, he wondered if they would ever have any true peace in their lives. She was beginning to fill the void left in his soul when Eva died. It wasn't love yet but who could say what was in the future for them.

Despite his reputation as a hard ass, Bennison was showing genuine compassion for Billy and the others from the two tribes. His investment was precarious at the moment but he still had total faith in the project. When Billy asked to see him, he had a pretty good idea what the conversation was going to be about.

"Thanks for seeing me Aubrey. I want to give you a personal update on the project. The guys are making real progress and we are almost back to where we were before the bombing. Worst case, we will be six months behind our targets, assuming nothing else comes up."

Wilson got up and poured each of them three fingers of single malt. "Ice?" he asked and Billy said yes.

"Thanks for the update. I get daily reports so this visit wasn't really necessary unless you have something else on your mind."

Billy took a sip of the scotch and smiled. "You're pretty perceptive. I do have something else I need to discuss with you if you don't mind."

"Let me guess. It has something to do with the bombing"

"Yes it does, but what I am about to tell you must stay between us only. Shan, my father, no one is to know. Understood?" Bennison nodded his agreement. "I need to hear you say it Aubrey."

"What we discuss will remain our secret. Are you happy now?"

"Before he died, the man that attacked me in the hospital gave me a name…I am sure he named the person behind the bombing and attempt on my life. He said the name "Drummond".

Bennison did not act at all surprised. "I had my suspicions. I know Damon is a spoiled and arrogant little prick but I am not convinced he has the brains or the balls to pull this off. It may have been his idea but I doubt he came up with the plan and hired the people on his own."

Billy listened but nothing Bennison said made any difference. "You may be right but I don't give a shit. Before this is over Drummond and whoever helped him will wish I died in that hospital."

"Have another drink. You need to relax and think everything through before you go off and get yourself in serious trouble." Aubrey added ice to Billy's glass and poured a stout refill.

"I need your help getting some hardware. I have a list of what I need." He handed him the slip of paper and Aubrey studied it carefully.

"From what's on this list, it looks like you want to start a war. I'm not an arms dealer Billy. Nevada is an open-carry state but you need a license to carry a concealed weapon…and you need to be a resident which you are not."

"Come on Aubrey. I'm not stupid. I know a man of your stature and importance can get things done…regardless of the law. Will you help me or not?"

"Billy if I help you, I cannot afford to have any blowback on me or my business. You have to promise me no one will get hurt unless its them or you." Without waiting for an answer, he took out one of his business cards and wrote something on the back and signed it.

"Go to Spurlock's Gun Shop in Henderson. Ask for John and hand him this card. Now get out of here before I change my mind. Oh yeah, bring lots of cash."

"Thank you Aubrey. You have my word none of this will land on your door step."

Billy walked back to his pickup before reading what was on the card. It said '*Give this man whatever he needs. Aubrey'*.

It was a short twenty-minute drive to Henderson which was really just a suburb of Las Vegas. After pulling in to the Spurlock's parking lot, Billy took one last look at the list he put together: Glock 19; four boxes of 9mm hollow points; Mossberg 12-gauge pump shotgun; one box of 12-gauge buck shot; and Bushnell binoculars.

The shop was crowded and Billy waited patiently while one of the salesmen finished up and turned to Billy. "What can I do for you?" he asked.

"I need to see John. Is he in today?"

"John's busy with another customer. I'll be glad to help you."

"Thanks but I really need to see John if you don't mind." The salesman shrugged his shoulders and called out for John, who walked up a few minutes later.

"John, thanks for helping me. A mutual friend told me I should only deal with you." Billy handed the business card to John and then gave him his shopping list.

John looked at Billy's list and entered some figures into his pocket calculator. "Well mister I must say you have a powerful friend in your camp. I'm pretty sure I have all of this in stock. I figure you're looking at around $3,000 give or take."

"Not a problem," Billy answered. "I'm going to need a shoulder holster for the Glock and some extra clips as well."

"Fine but you'll have to come back after closing. I can't have a crowd around when we do this. Too many questions might be asked and neither of us want that now, do we?"

Billy left and called Aubrey. "I just left your friend John. He'll have what I need ready after they close tonight. I need one last favor, though. It's going to cost more than I have with me and I don't want to drive all the way back to Laughlin. Can I borrow a couple thousand?"

"Not a problem. I'll call down to the Sands cashier office. Pick up as much as you need but this is our last conversation for a while." Aubrey wanted as much distance between what Billy did and himself as possible.

Spurlock's closed at five but Billy was told to wait until six so that all the employees were gone. At the agreed time, John stepped outside and motioned for Billy to enter the shop. Everything Billy ordered was neatly packed in a long zippered weapons bag. "Here you go. You might want to look and make sure I didn't miss anything."

Billy inventoried the items and found a tactical flashlight which was not on his list. "I don't remember listing the flashlight, John."

"My gift. You might need it." John answered. Billy handed over $3,000 in cash and shook the hand of his new friend. "Good luck whoever you are. Don't make me read about you in the papers tomorrow."

CHAPTER 26

Damon was happy to be back in his penthouse suite. Elena and the kids moved out after the divorce settlement was completed and booked a three-week cruise for the three of them, allowing her attorney time to search for an appropriate residence for her.

There had been no contact between Damon and Jackie for weeks. The waters appeared to be calm and the Palace was getting off life support and making money again. Zerilli's first act as managing partner was to move Mark over to help Jill run the day-to-day operations. Damon's role had been reduced to a figurehead with no power. He still had a vote but would always be overruled by the rest of the board.

Zerilli's second act was to have the Drummond name removed from the property marquee. Damon fought hard against this and, after much deliberation and convincing by Jill, Jackie rescinded his demand. She believed that the Drummond brand retained some of the credulity associated with its patriarch Wilfred Drummond. If Damon stayed in the shadows and did nothing stupid, the brand should continue to create value.

Damon spent most of his days on the golf course or in one of the Palace bars. He had his regular stable of show girls that were constantly on his arm and in his bed. He rarely went to Vegas to avoid any contact with Aubrey Bennison or any of his associates.

The day after Billy's shopping spree at the gun shop, Damon was on the links enjoying a round with three strangers that were looking for a player for their foursome. Damon proposed playing for $100 per hole and the group accepted his challenge…and cleaned his clock. After the round, Damon lingered in the bar before taking his shower in the member's locker room.

"Hey Rodrigo, fire up the sauna for me. I need to sweat out all the tequila in my system." The locker room attendant never liked the arrogant millionaire but there was always the possibility of a big tip so he played the game.

"Sure thing Mister Drummond. How about a nice massage afterwards?"

"Perfect. If I fall asleep just leave me on the table." Damon removed his clothes and stepped in the shower while Rodrigo got the sauna ready for him. He was the only member still in the locker room.

"All set Mister Drummond. Buzz me when you are ready for your massage." Rodrigo poured water on the rocks and left.

When Damon entered the sauna room he wrapped himself in a towel and sat on the wooden bench, allowing his body to purge itself of all the toxins it had absorbed. Twice he added water to the rocks to sustain the intensity of the heat. After 15 minutes, he stepped out to allow his body to cool down, then reentered for another 15 minutes which was his maximum.

After the sauna, he returned to the shower to wash off all of the perspiration and then toweled himself dry in anticipation of the next step…a deep muscle massage. He walked to the massage area and pressed the buzzer to call the masseuse. His favorite was Anna, a beauty from Thailand that had incredible hands and technique that, for a sizeable tip, would include a *Happy Ending*.

Damon knew the drill. He removed his towel and laid face down on the padded table. After several minutes, he called out for Anna and continued to wait until he heard the door open and Anna's footsteps as she walked to the table, standing over him. "What the hell took you so long?" he asked, expecting a sincere apology. Instead, he felt a heavy weight on the back of his neck, restricting air flow. “What the fuck?” he gasped as he struggled to sit up. He was allowed to turn his head and saw the barrel of a Glock aimed between his eyes.

“Who are you? Rodrigo, Rodrigo!” he screamed in desperation.

All he heard in response was silence…then a sinister whisper coming from the hooded person holding the gun. “I know! You are a worthless piece of shit and it’s time you paid for the misery you created for so many people…including your wife and kids. What I need you to tell me is who your partner was. I know a fucking worm like you doesn’t have the balls to blow up a casino or try and kill someone recovering in the hospital. I will only ask you one more time, Damon. Who was your partner?”

“If I tell you, I’m a dead man. Then my wife and kids will be next. These people have no conscious. They kill like it’s a game…no remorse.”

Billy grabbed Damon’s right wrist and forced his hand down on the table. With one swing, he smashed the butt of the Glock into the hand, shattering more bones than you could count. Damon screamed in agony and held his bleeding hand like it was a newborn baby. “You crazy fuck! I need a doctor…now!”

"Looks like your handicap just jumped ten strokes. Are your ready for round two?" Billy grabbed Damon's other wrist and positioned the left hand for the same blow as the right.

"Wait, for God's sake!" Damon screamed out. "Why do you care about this shit? Who are you anyhow?" Billy laughed, then slammed the gun in to Damon's other hand.

"I'm still waiting for an answer to my question," Billy answered, then removed his ski mask so Damon could see who his tormentor was. Damon screamed again in pain and was now crying like a baby. "Everyone told me you were a whiny little bitch, Damon. Guess they were right. OK…now we move to your feet."

"ENOUGH!" Damon screamed. "Jackie Zerilli's people were responsible. Do you know who he is because if you don't, you are about to learn a hard lesson on who a real bad ass is."

"The mob guy? Did he authorize the bombing and the knife attack? How did you get mixed up with him?" Billy was genuinely confused. It made no sense unless the Zerilli family was pumping money into Damon's companies.

"How much are you paying them? Do you think they will just go away after they clean up your shit? They are going to suck every penny from you and then someone will find your ass buried in the desert."

Damon pleaded for the beating to stop. "What choice do I have? Between my wife and those fucking Indians, I was losing everything. Zerilli threw me a life preserver and I took it. I can't rewind this tape."

"Take a hard look at me. I'm one of those fucking Indians that you almost killed in that bomb attack. I'm also that fucking Indian that you tried to have killed while I was recovering in the hospital. And I'm also that fucking Indian that just crushed both your hands and will put you in a wheel chair for the rest of your ugly life…unless you help me get to Jackie Zerilli."

"I'll do whatever you want. Just get me to a hospital…please!" Billy called 9-1-1 then told Damon what he wanted him to do. By the time the ambulance arrived Billy was long gone.

* * *

When word leaked out to the papers, Damon was covered up with reporters asking for a statement on how he got injured and if there was any foul play involved. With both of his hands bandaged, it was difficult to come up with an explanation that held water so he settled on burning his hands while barbequing on his patio. Everyone bought into the explanation except two people…Aubrey Bennison and Jackie Zerilli.

"Do you want to tell me the truth or do I have to finish what that prick started?" Jackie was in no mood for a prolonged discussion.

"I was going to fill you in. It's a little hard to dial a phone when you can't use your hands. If you would have finished the job you started none of this would have happened. The fucker came to my club for God's sake." Damon was not lying this time. "He's a goddamn animal, Jackie. He knows what happened and wants revenge. Maybe we can buy him off, I don't know, but if he is still breathing he'll be on my ass."

"You are a weak pussy. You think I should pay this guy off so he doesn't bust your balls? Time to grow a pair rich boy."

Damon needed to bait the hook. "We need to talk. I have an idea how we can make this go away. Remember, he's fucking up your investments as well as mine. Give me a chance to lay it out for you, OK?" Damon was hoping they would meet at Jackie's place at the Desert Inn which would give the Indian lots of places to set an ambush.

"Let me think about it. I'll call you back."

* * *

"I don't want to know the details, Billy." Bennison saw the reports and had no difficulty putting the pieces together. "My only question is why didn't he call the police and just get you arrested for attempted murder or something?"

"I gave him a chance to save his ass and hand me the real muscle behind the bombing. It's a name you will recognize, Aubrey. Trust me these are bad people and they won't stop until they put us in the ground or out of business."

"And you are willing to risk everything to get revenge? You could lose more than your life Billy. Think about your family, your people. Is it really worth a blood bath?"

Billy had considered everything that Aubrey said. "Aubrey, you know I have the utmost respect for you. We could have never gotten this far without your support. For that I will be forever grateful. But if all of this turns to shit you are still a billionaire and life will go on. This will just be a speed bump for you. Sitting Bull once said that the white man broke every promise made to the Indians except one…they said they would take our land…and they took it.

The Lakota had 60 million acres guaranteed by the Treaty of 1868. Today they have 5 million acres…no gold…no buffalo…nothing. I have fought in your country's wars. I have killed many to protect your way of life. Now I will kill to protect my way of life."

CHAPTER 27

Jackie Zerilli did not live this long by being stupid. His instincts had proven correct over and over and they were telling him now that he needed to be extra cautious. He decided to meet Damon at the Clark County Wetlands Park at the eastern edge of the county where East Tropicana Blvd. transitioned into South Broadbent Blvd. Should the need arise, it was also less than a mile from the Las Vegas Wash.

He instructed Jimmy Gallanto to take one of his guys and find a good spot for the meet. Zerilli always liked the "Powell Doctrine" that advocated using overwhelming force to subdue an adversary. It didn't fail Colin Powell and never failed Jackie either.

Billy was back in Laughlin when he got the call he was expecting from Drummond. "I was about to give up on you. Is the meeting set up?"

"We are to meet in two days at the Clark County Wetlands Park. There is a pedestrian trail from the main parking lot that leads to Turtle Pond. Another half mile gets you to the Wildlife Viewing Blind. He'll be there just before the park closes at 4 PM."

"Looks like he picked a meeting place that gives him the element of surprise if needed. My guess is he suspects you are setting him up to save your ass. I also suspect that the plan does not include you walking away alive. He will kill you Damon and anyone else that gets involved."

"Which is why I will be miles away when you meet him. I've done my part like you asked me."

"Sorry, but if he doesn't see you he will bail out before I can get to him. You will be there with a big grin on your face. Don't be late."

* * *

Billy was ready for his rendezvous with the Zerilli family. He planned on getting to the park around noon and recon the entire area. He assumed that Jackie would not come alone and would have plenty of muscle with him. Damon was to arrive at the agreed upon time.

Billy sat with Shan and bared his soul. "Please don't try to talk be out of doing this brother. We have come too far to give up on our dream. My father is old and has given his life to improving the lives of our people. You have been like a son to him…a better son than I have been and he loves you…as I do."

Shan knew Billy was going up against his own Goliath and with not much more than a slingshot. "Let me send some warriors to go with you. These kids read the history books and long for the days when the young men of the tribe rode out to do battle. Like you, they are not afraid."

"Shan, they may not be afraid, but going to war is not glorious or noble…it is bloody and people get hurt. These boys are our future. I won't put them in harm's way to fight my battle."

Shan would not give up. "What about Karen? I know you have strong feelings for her. Without you she may wander away from the life you gave her. That would be tragic, Billy."

Billy had thought a lot about Karen…the new Karen that was thriving with the Clan. He decided to call her before he left. It might be the last time they spoke and he had things to say to her. "You're right Shan. Karen is important to me and has become part of our family. One thing I am sure of though, she would support my decision 100%. She's a warrior and proved it."

Shan helped Billy with his gear and they shared a pipe, like their ancestors would do before battle.

Afterwards, Shan had one of the women apply war paint to Billy's face and arms. He was ready.

As he made the drive to the meeting place, he thought about what he wanted to say to Karen. He didn't want to scare her but she needed to know how he felt about her and his dreams for the future…a future that would include her. He saw a Circle K with a payphone and pulled over.

"Red Bison Souvenirs and Gifts…can I help you?" As cute and feminine as she looked, Karen had a deep gravelly voice that just made her sexier to him…totally opposite of Eva.

"Hi Karen…keeping busy?"

"Billy, I thought you were coming back this week. Is anything wrong?" Karen had a sixth sense when it came to Billy and could tell from his voice he had something on his mind.

"Sure, I'm still coming but something came up that I have to take care of. No big deal. Have they taught you how to make Wojabi yet? It's the quickest way to my heart."

Karen laughed. "By the time you get here I will be the best Wojabi maker in the tribe. So, did you call to bust my chops about my cooking ability or do you just miss me?"

"I do miss you Karen. Since I got out of the hospital I've been doing a lot of thinking…about us and our future. I was always a loner and never really got into the traditions of my people. I played things fast and loose and now everything is different. I think you'll agree that you are different too…in a good way. I had someone I really cared about taken from me and until I make things right, I can't fill that empty space in my heart. You can fill that space but I need a little more time."

"Billy I thought what we did in Detroit finished that chapter. Am I missing something?" She feared the answer to that question but needed to know.

"I'm convinced the people that killed Eva were also responsible for the bombing and trying to kill me in the hospital. In Detroit, we took out someone that was mid-level at best. I want the guy pushing the buttons…the guy at the top of the food chain. I hope you can understand. I need to do this one last thing and if I make it through, I want you to be my wife."

"Wow Billy. That's a lot for a girl to digest. You know I love you and I support what you need to do but is it really necessary? Why not just come back to Oklahoma and forget about the casino if it's going to get you killed or back in the hospital. Your father will understand. I know it."

"I'm sorry but that is not an option that I can accept. Pray for me Karen. I love you." Billy hung up and returned to his truck. One more hour until show time.

* * *

When Billy arrived at the Wetland Park the place was packed with visitors...mostly snow birds that were vacationing in Las Vegas and looking for a cheap diversion. At the entrance booth, he was given a map of the area with detailed illustrations of the various hiking trails. He located the trail leading to Turtle Pond and took a leisurely pace that ended at the Wildlife Viewing Blind.

The area was secluded with excellent site lines of 180 degrees, providing the onlooker great opportunities to study the various birds that visited the Pond and the adjacent Las Vegas Wash. Billy found a spot hidden by several cottonwood trees. He rolled a good size rock to the right spot and created shooting perch. He had two hours to kill and wished he had something to read. Instead, he used his seven-inch recon knife, a keepsake from the war, to whittle away at some limbs and branches.

Expecting Damon to arrive around 3:45, Billy was startled when he heard footsteps coming down the path from the Pond. He used his binoculars to identify two men, both in leisure suits, slowly walking into the Blind area. A check of his watch confirmed it was 3:30. Each man took a position on the perimeter and both were carrying assault rifles and making no effort to hide them. How they got in with the weapons was a good question. A minute later another man, appearing to be unarmed, came into the circle and sat on one of the tourist benches.

"Just us and the birds boss. No sign of your boy yet." Billy didn't recognize the speaker but he was clearly talking to the man in charge. Once Damon confirmed it was Zerilli, there would be no turning back. Billy decided to take out the muscle first…then Zerilli. He wished he had his old sniper rifle but the 12 gauge should handle the job. The shotgun already had a round of buck shot chambered so there would be no racking sound to tip them off.

Almost on cue, Damon walked in to the circle, brushing leaves and dust from his cashmere jacket. "Jesus Jackie, could you have picked a shittier place to meet?" Jackie could see the nervousness in Jackie's face.

"I love nature, what can I say," Jackie answered sarcastically. "Boys, make sure our friend isn't packing, not that he would have a clue or the balls to shoot a gun." One of the men pointed his carbine at Damon while the other one patted him down, then nodded to his boss.

"So Mister Drummond…come sit next to me. Please tell me what is so important you had to tell me in person. You know that makes me nervous and one thing you never want is to see me nervous."

Damon hoped that Billy was there and listening. "Jackie I've been thinking that maybe you should take over everything…just buy me out. I'm sure we can agree on a fair price. I'm not cut out for all the shit that's gone down with the Indians. I'm just in the way."

Jackie laughed and the two men joined in, having no idea what was so funny but he was the boss. "So Humpty Dumpty wants to jump off the wall. The massive Drummond ego has been nothing but a smoke screen. You are pathetic. I should break your knees for wasting my time. I can have everything without paying you another fucking dime. What are you going to do, call the cops? I don't think so little rich boy. Come on fellas' we need to punish this piece of shit for taking me away from my golf game."

As the two me advanced towards Damon he lost it. "Billy…where the fuck are you!" he screamed stopping the men in their tracks. That was Billy's cue and he fired once, hitting the taller man in the knee cap, almost severing the leg entirely.

As the other man turned with his rifle leveled at where the shot came from, Billy ran out into the clearing and fired again at the second man. At that close range, there was no option to wound…only to kill and the buckshot ripped through the man's body armor, sending him six feet into the woods. He was dead.

By then Jackie was on his feet grabbing Damon as a shield while he pulled a snubby .38 from his ankle holster. "Hold it cock sucker! Put the shotgun down or I'll cap this motherfucker! Jimmy, how bad are you hit?" The man with the leg wound just moaned. He would be no help to Jackie and Billy knew it.

Billy put the shotgun down and stepped to where he could see the man on the ground as well as Zerilli. He was far enough away from Jackie that he calculated the mobster would be unable to make a clean shot with one hand holding Damon. Billy had plenty of time to pull the Glock and get two rounds into his target…one of which might end up being Damon Drummond.

"Hey relax. You have the gun not me. Why don't you let Damon go and just walk away? I promise I'll call for an ambulance for your friend. Us Cherokee are civilized…thanks to you and President Grant. Do you like my war paint? I put this on just for you. I think the colors go pretty well with my complexion. What do you think?"

Jackie's arm holding the gun was shaking, another factor to consider before Billy made his move. "You are one crazy fucker. All of this could have been avoided if you and your old man would have accepted Califano's offer. We just wanted a place where we could clean some cash without the feds noticing. So here we are with some broad dead in Detroit and all this mess here in Laughlin. I've also lost some good earners, Geronimo because of you. I even think you owe me an apology. How about it? Just say you're sorry, get on your horse and ride back to Oklahoma. Have some fire water around the campfire and tell the tribe all about your Las Vegas adventure. I'll take care of this piece of shit for you too. My gift."

Billy was about to explode with rage but measured every breath, every move before acting. "That is a very generous offer. Can I take a minute to think about it?" Before Jackie could answer the Glock was drawn and aimed at Zerilli's head. "Ooops, times up. My answer is kiss my red ass."

"I'll kill him! I'm not fucking around! If you shoot you may hit Damon. Is that what you want?" Jackie could barely keep the gun aimed.

"Actually, I do." Billy answered, putting the first round into Damon's right eye and the second into Jackie's chest. Both men dropped to the ground. It was over for Damon but Jackie was holding on, blood gushing from the belly wound…a very painful and slow way to die.

As Zerilli lay bleeding out, Billy put on his gloves and retrieved one of the assault rifles. He checked that the clip was full with a round in the chamber then walked up to the man he shot with the 12 gauge. "So Jimmy, is it? I would love to stick around and chat but those gunshots have probably got the cavalry on the way. So let's just say goodbye." A burst of .223 rounds ripped his chest open and punctured his heart.

"Well Jackie I think my work is done here. Ouch, that wound looks really bad but don't worry, it'll all be over in a few minutes. Before I go, I want you to know that broad you had killed in Detroit…her name was Eva. She was my fiancé…and she was carrying my son in her belly. Have a nice day."

CHAPTER 28

Billy left his truck where it was parked and walked, going east through the Las Vegas Wash. The water in the wash was running from a recent rain storm and he stopped to clean the paint from his face and arms. He then found a spot where the earth was soft and moist and dug a hole to bury his shotgun and the gloves he had worn. He kept the Glock and the binoculars and began the mile hike to the main highway where he was able to catch a ride to the same Circle K he had visited earlier.

As he stood at the pay phone, he saw the procession of flashing lights approaching then passing him on the way to the Preserve. He hoped no one saw him but he couldn't be certain. Best to assume the worst, he thought. "Shan, it's Billy. I sure could use a ride. It's been an interesting afternoon."

Shan hadn't heard any news reports and didn't want to ask any questions on the phone. Billy told him where he was and Shan sent a member of the tribe to pick him up. Two hours later Billy was sitting in Shan's office with a cold beer in his hand. KSNV was broadcasting the report of the shootings at the Clark County Wetlands Park.

"I assume this is your handiwork. They say they found four bodies but would not release the names yet. Billy there is no good ending to this story. You know that, I hope. You'll be safe here for a while but sooner or later you will have to leave. I'm sorry but I must do what is best for my people…my tribe. Harboring a fugitive is against tribal law, not just the white man's."

"What I did was done for all of us Shan. There were no other options that would have kept us safe. Sooner or later they were going to squeeze us out of our land and what we are building. I've read that chapter in our history too many times and you're right…there is no good ending to that story. Sooner or later we must say ENOUGH! And that's what I did."

A few days later two detectives from the LVMD showed up at the reservation. They ran the plates on the abandoned F-150 which was registered to the Fort Mohave Tribe. They were waiting for Shan who was returning to his office after lunch. "Gentlemen, how can I help our men in blue?"

After introducing themselves, the lead detective showed Shan a picture of Billy's blue pickup, clearly showing the license plate number. "Our records indicate this vehicle is owned by your tribe and was found at the scene of a multiple homicide. Can you explain how this truck made its way to a crime scene Mister Williams?"

Shan studied the picture for a second then handed it back. "Are you sure this is one of ours? We have so many trucks running around here. I can't be expected to know every one of them."

"Well maybe this can jog your memory. We have lifted several sets of prints and guess what? They match a Mister Billy Whitehorse. Is he a member of your tribe because we would really love to chat with him." He handed Shan a second photo…this one of Billy in uniform with all his medals from Vietnam displayed. "Do you recognize the man in this picture?"

Shan looked at it then put it on his desk. "Well you know the old saying, they all look alike to me."

"Don't be a smart-ass Mister Williams. Do you know this man or not? If you don't help me, I'll haul every one of your men in for finger printing and who knows what other charges we might come up with?"

"I know him. Every Indian knows him. He is a decorated War Hero and served his country in your horrible war in Vietnam. Last I heard he was playing in a band right here in Las Vegas. Pretty good too I hear. I have no idea how his fingerprints ended up in that truck. Maybe he was friends with one of our people. That's about all I can tell you."

The detective picked up the two pictures and motioned to his partner. "OK, that's all for now. We'll be back to talk to your people if we don't get any more leads. Make sure no one leaves the county for the next couple of weeks."

Billy watched as they drove off. "They haven't made the connection to Oklahoma yet but they will be watching the airport and train station…maybe the bus terminal too. They have your picture Billy and you haven't changed that much." Shan's wheels were turning but he was unable to see any scenario that could get Billy out of town unless it was by car.

"Looks like my only option is to get a car and drive back to Tulsa but I will need ID to get a rental and I assume you won't donate another tribal truck to my charitable foundation."

"Sorry Billy but giving you one from our fleet is out of the question. You really need to call Karen and your father but not from here. My guess is they will be tapping our phones as soon as they get a court order signed. You really don't have much time."

"OK, I have one option but it's a long shot at best. I gave my old car to a friend when I moved to Oklahoma. If he still has it, maybe he'll let me take it back. He'll really be sticking his neck out but he's a good man and just might help me out."

* * *

Willy Deville wrapped up his band's gig at the Stardust and was sitting in his apartment when Billy's call came in. "Dude…are you OK? Cops paid me a visit a few days ago looking for you. I said I hadn't seen you for months and that you had quit the band. What kind of trouble have you gotten into my brother?"

"The worst kind Willy. I need to get out of town pronto but they will be watching for me at the airport and I can't get a rental without ID. Do you see where I'm coming from?"

"I guess I do and you are one lucky dude. I still have the Trans Am. Haven't driven it much since you gave it to me but you can have it back if you want. No problem. I hope it can get you to wherever you need to go."

They agreed that Willy would leave the Trans Am in the Albertson's parking lot in Boulder City. The keys would be on the driver's side front tire. "I'll even fill the fucking tank for you…how's that for friendship?"

“I have no words Willy. I can never repay you but someday I’ll pop up in your rear view mirror and we will talk about old times together…I promise.”

When Billy returned from his phone call to Willy, Shan told him to sit down. He had some news. “That detective just called me back. They know about the Red Bison Clan and that your father runs it. They have called the Oklahoma Highway Patrol with your description and I expect they will be knocking on Wilson’s door by the end of the week. I’m sorry Billy. If you try to return to the reservation they will catch you and bring you back to Nevada. Have you talked to your father or Karen yet?”

“Shit…I can’t catch a break. No, I was going to call them and tell them I was on my way. Willy is dropping my old car off in Boulder City tomorrow. I can’t put my family in danger, Shan. They’ve been through enough. I need to think this through before I get the car. Can you give me another day? Please.”

Billy returned to the old Airstream he was living in on the reservation and opened a beer. He tried to think of anyone, even fellow vets he had served with, that could help him out. It took a full six-pack before the name of Raymond Givens came to mind. Ray was one of the men he saved outside of Hue the day he earned most of his decorations for valor. Billy had actually held Ray's exposed heart in his hands as he massaged it to keep it beating until the medivac could land. If anyone owed a favor to Billy it was him.

All Billy remembered about his brother-in-arms was that he had worked on his family's fishing boat in San Pedro when he got drafted after high school. Billy checked an old map of the United States he found in the trailer. San Pedro was about a four or five-hour drive from Las Vegas. It would be the only option that made any sense.... if Ray was still living there.

In the morning, Billy filled his old duffel with clothes and other items, including the Glock that was now his only friend. He walked to Shan's office to say goodbye. "I need a ride to Boulder City to get my old car. After that I am putting all of this in my rear-view mirror. I can't call my father from here but I'll find a payphone somewhere. You've been a good friend, Shan…all of you. It's better if you don't know where I am going. If I get lucky someday I'll see you again."

Shan called someone and a truck pulled up, Billy's ride to Boulder City. "You will be missed my brother. If we get this casino built it will be on the foundation your courage provided. Our children will learn about Billy

Whitehorse and books will be written by our people. You will live forever. Be safe."

Billy almost didn't recognize his old car. The black paint was fading badly from exposure to the desert sun and the leather seats were cracked badly. He should have gotten sheep skins when he had the chance. The keys were on the tire as expected and the fuel gauge showed he had a full tank. Billy unpacked the Glock and a spare clip then threw his bag in the back seat…barely wide enough to hold the large duffel. He turned the ignition key and the big 6.6L V-8 roared to life.

After one last check of his map, Billy pulled on to west bound 515, then south on I-15. He hoped he had enough fuel to reach Barstow where he planned to make phone calls to his father, Karen and, hopefully Raymond Givens. As he crossed the Nevada border into California, his radio reception became intermittent so he dug into the console and found a cassette of some of his favorite Hendrix tunes… *"Will I live tomorrow…well I just can't say. But I know for sure…I'm gonna live today."*

CHAPTER 29

The old Trans Am was running on fumes when Billy pulled in to the Flying J truck stop in Barstow. A line of 18-wheelers was waiting to fill their tanks with diesel fuel. A number of normal gas pumps were open and Billy filled up and paid cash inside.

The Flying J had a spacious dining area with plenty of truckers sitting at the long counters enjoying the local cuisine. Billy used the men's room and found several shower stalls, all occupied with men like himself, eager to wash away the road grime.

After eating a cheeseburger and fries, he asked the cashier for several dollars in quarters and went to the bank of pay phone booths where he could sit and make his calls. His first call was to the information operator. "I need a listing for Raymond Givens in San Pedro. I also need an address if you have it."

After spelling the last name, the operator came back on the line. "I show no listing for Raymond Givens. I did find a listing for Givens Marine Fleet. Would you like that number?" Billy asked for that listing and wrote it down on a napkin he had borrowed.

Before trying the business listing he thought it was time to confront what he did with his father and Karen. He called the souvenir shop first. "Karen, it's Billy. I'm sorry I haven't called you sooner but I've been kinda busy."

"My God Billy we've been worried sick. Shan wouldn't give us any information so all we have is what we have seen on television news. Is it true? Are you responsible for those killings at the Wildlife Preserve?"

"Listen Karen, I'm calling the shop number because Shan is convinced they are tapping the phones at both Reservations. That's why Shan couldn't give you any information. Believe me, without his help I would be behind bars or dead."

"Can you tell me where you are? Are you on your way back to Oklahoma? I miss you so much Billy. I cry myself to sleep every night. Your father stopped eating. He is so weak and frail. I am worried about his health. He needs his son to come home."

"I wish that was possible but it's not. The feds are on their way to talk to my dad if they haven't shown up already. They will be watching everyone that comes or goes there…including you. I need to disappear for a while…until they stop looking for me, which may take a while given the people that died in that park. To answer your question…yes, I killed those pieces of shit and I have no regrets. I understand I didn't have the right to decide who should live or die but our God left it to me and I did what I truly believe was necessary."

Karen began to weep uncontrollably. "So are you saying you are going away…for how long? Jesus Billy, I need something to hold on to. Something that can give me hope to hang on and not give up…give up on us."

"Don't give up, Karen. Don't give up on all you've accomplished. It wasn't me, it was you that got us through hell in Detroit. I can deal with whatever is ahead of me if I know you will be there when I come home. Please promise me that, Karen."

"I'll be here Billy. I'll be here. Please come home to me." She heard the line go dead.

* * *

"Givens Marine…can you hold please?" It took Billy a moment to recover from his tearful farewell with Karen, then he placed the call that could save his life. "Thanks for holding. How I can I help you?"

"I'd like to speak to Ray Givens please. My name is Whitehorse. We were in Nam together."

"Just a sec…he may have left already." Billy waited while whoever answered went to get Ray.

"This is Ray. Who's calling again?"

"Billy Whitehorse is calling you piece of shit. How are you?"

"Are you fucking kidding me...Billy Whitehorse? You are the last person I expected to wash up on my dock. Have to admit you are having your fifteen minutes of fame old buddy."

"Don't believe everything you read, Ray. I'm calling because I need your help. I'm on my way to see you if you will give me the chance. Can you give an old friend a couple hours of your time?"

"Sure, but you need to hurry. I'm heading out to sea day after tomorrow. Will be gone for a couple of weeks if the tuna haven't taken a vacation." He gave Billy the address of his shop and said he looked forward to seeing him. Billy would be on his doorstep in a couple of hours.

By the time Billy arrived at Givens Marine the place was closed for the day. He pulled the Trans Am around the back where the expansive parking area was littered with fishing gear that was going to be used the following day. Sitting like a regal queen at dockside was a massive Seiner that had to be over 200 feet long. It was named "The Gallant". Billy was no sailor but knew a boat this size was meant to stay at sea for a long time, filling its nets till they were about to burst before returning to port.

In the darkness, Billy could smell the salty breeze coming in and the sound of the water lapping against the wooden pier was the perfect recipe to bring on sleep. He did his best to get comfortable in his car for the night and went out like a light.

The next morning, he was awakened by someone pounding on the hood of his car. "Hey buddy this isn't a camp ground. Get the fuck out of here before we call the cops." Billy sat up and opened the door, stepping out in full view of the man who's heart he had cradled in his hands a thousand years ago.

"Nice to see you too Mister Givens," Billy said as the two men hugged like kids on the playground.

"Come on inside and get some coffee in you." Ray answered, leading Billy across the lot to the small building that served as the world headquarters of Givens Marine. "Marie could you pour me and my old friend some of that firewater you call coffee?" The young girl with blonde hair halfway down her back laughed and pulled two mugs from the pantry.

"Here you go," she said, placing the steaming mugs on Ray's beat up metal desk. "Are you going to introduce me to your friend?"

"Sorry…Marie this is an old army buddy I haven't seen since he saved my ass in Hue when the hippies were here making love in the street and smoking dope. Billy this is my daughter Marie, the best sailor in my crew of misfits."

"Nice to meet you Marie. Someday I hope you'll introduce me to your real father cause this old turd couldn't make someone as beautiful as you."

After making small talk with Marie, she excused herself so they could visit in private. "Ray, what you've read in the papers about me is mostly true. It's a very long story but please understand I did what I had to do for my family and tribe. If you want to call the police go ahead but before you do, think about the man who was your friend back in the shit. All we had was each other. We didn't fight for God and Country…we fought for the man standing next to us. We believed and trusted each other. I need that same trust now. I need your help."

"You don't look like much a seaman Billy, but if you're willing to bust your ass I can use a good man. All you need to do is keep up with Marie. If you can do that you'll fit in just fine. Welcome to the crew of The Gallant…the finest tuna seiner in the pacific."

CHAPTER 30

Two years later...

With the death of Damon Drummond, the Palace went into bankruptcy where the court discovered that the Zerilli family was the majority stock holder. Jackie's heirs wanted no part of the business and allowed the casino and resort to be sold to Aubrey Bennison for ten cents on the dollar. He was the only bidder.

With the completion of the Mystic River Resort six months earlier, Aubrey offered the two tribes the same ownership position in the Palace that he had in their property. Wilson was seriously ill and unable to participate in the meeting but gave Shan the authority to sign on behalf of the Red Bison Clan. The Palace was renamed the Moon Shadow Resort and Casino and began to thrive, just as its sister casino had been doing since its opening.

After significant renovations were completed, it was time to introduce the Moon Shadow to the world. Aubrey located the agent for Cat Stevens, now known as Yusuf Islam, to appear at the opening…primarily to sing his hit "Moon Shadow". After much coaxing, the reclusive singer identified with the plight of the American Indians and agreed to perform.

In her exit interview, Jill Beauville gave Aubrey a convincing case to keep her on board. Shan also met with her and agreed that she had a skill set unique to the gaming industry and also knew where all the bodies were buried in the old Drummond organization. Armed with those endorsements, she took over the planning and implementation of the re-opening event. In addition to Cat Stevens, she succeeded in booking other established rock acts like Van Morrison, and Steely Dan who were finishing up engagements at other Las Vegas venues.

As he did for the ground breaking of the Mystic River, Bennison was able to buy the attendance of the Governor who was locked in a heated re-election battle and needed positive exposure…and Bennison's money. The event was set for September 6th which coincided with the annual celebration of the signing in 1839 of the Constitution of the Cherokee Nation. It was imperative that the Red Bison Clan be represented and Wilson asked Karen to assume that honor…even though she was not a native-born Cherokee.

"Wilson, I'm not the one who should represent your Clan. It should be you or one of your nieces or nephews.

I'm a white girl from Chicago. I would be an embarrassment to your people."

Wilson was now confined to his bed or a wheel chair when he had the energy. He motioned for Karen to remove the oxygen mask he was wearing…he had something to say. "You, more than anyone, represents the best of our people. You are kind, honest, hardworking, reliable and, most important, my son loved you. You have come to us with broken wings and I have watched you heal yourself and embrace the ways of a people you knew nothing about. I love you like a daughter…we all love you Karen."

As Karen was finishing up packing for the flight to Las Vegas, one of the matriarchs of the clan brought her a package she was to take to the ceremony. After she left, Karen opened it and found a ceremonial garment worn by the women of the tribe for special events. It fit perfectly. She would wear it proudly.

* * *

Well it's a marvelous night for a moon dance, with the stars up above in your eyes… Van Morrison and his band were kicking off the celebration as the attendees were finding their assigned tables. The stage had been set up outdoors, across from the Colorado River and the marina of the Mystic River. It was indeed a marvelous night for a moon dance.

A table had been set up for the hosts and other celebrities. After Van Morrison's set, Aubrey Bennison took the mike to introduce members of the two tribes that were now his partners. As he called their names, they took a seat at the main table to the applause of the audience. The final introduction was for the lone representative from the Red Bison Cherokee Clan. When Aubrey called Karen's name he stumbled. No one had ever told him her last name. "And from the Red Bison tribe from Oklahoma, please welcome Karen…ah… Karen Whitehorse."

No one was more surprised at the added surname than Karen. With the spotlight focused on her, the crowd gasped at the beauty of the woman and the outfit she was wearing. She looked every bit the Native American Princess that she had become.

To Aubrey's surprise, Karen took the mike from his hands. "Ladies and Gentlemen, tonight we not only celebrate the re-opening of this magnificent resort. We also honor the memory of the signing in 1839 of the Constitution of the Cherokee Nation. Our people had just endured the Trail of Tears and this new constitution declared horrors like that would never again descend upon

Native Americans. Sadly, we learned that signed pieces of paper cannot guaranty that the written words are honored. Our fight continued then and continues now.

One man who is not here with us sacrificed everything to insure this day would happen. His name is Billy Whitehorse. Please stand and join me in a moment of silence for this brave warrior." The crowed rose and, with bowed heads, gave Billy the respect he had always fought for. The silence was broken by a lone acoustic guitar…*"Oh, I'm bein' followed by a moon shadow, moon shadow, moon shadow--- / Leapin and hoppin' on a moon shadow, moon shadow, moon shadow--- / And if I ever lose my hands, lose my plough, lose my land, / Oh if I ever lose my hands, Oh if I won't have to work no more."*

EPILOGUE

It proved to be a magical evening for Karen. A line of young men hoped to get a chance to dance with her as Cat Stevens performed hit after hit followed by Steely Dan who, in the spirit of the event, did their best to surpass the previous performance.

Their encore number was "Riki Don't Lose That Number" and it was Aubrey Bennison that Karen chose to close the evening with on the dance floor. Despite Aubrey's age, he glided across the floor, cradling the young girl in his arms as though she was his daughter. Karen closed her eyes and became lost in the music. Sensing the emotion that was on display, the dance floor emptied leaving just the lone couple to bathe in that moment.

In the shadows, another pair of eyes were glued on the dancers. The man stood in the darkness and tears formed, slowly making their way down his weathered cheek. He wanted so much to be holding the young girl as he had done before. Maybe someday, he thought…but not this day.

"This problem - it is age old. To do what is right and save the day without destroying the very thing the day is lived for."

Christopher Pike

ABOUT THE AUTHOR

JIM FRISHKEY is an acclaimed author of nine fiction novels, many of which weave a narrative through historical events that launch the reader on an electrifying adventure he won't soon forget.

Inspired by a sympathetic educator in high school, Jim's talents as a writer surfaced after many years of experiences that would shape his life and perspective on the future.

Jim has an MBA; is a life-long musician; loves muscle cars and Janice, his editor wife of 45 years. He resides in a suburb of Dallas…but hates the Cowboys (Go Steelers!)

Beginning with "Spawn", his fourth novel, Jim introduced a memorable anti-hero that continued in "Shadows in the Mirror" and "Markov".

OTHER BOOKS BY JIM FRISHKEY

"Terminal Convergence"

"Jacks or Better"

"Return to Forever"

"Spawn"

"A Simple Man"

"Shadows in the Mirror"

"Markov"

Jimfrishkeyauthor.com